Bella

Other books by the author:

Stories of Love, Hope and Healing for All Ages

STOP Family Anxiety: A guide for anxiety disorders in parents, grandparents, teenagers and children of all ages

Depression: Light at the End of the Tunnel

The Third Generation

The Elephant's Footprint

The Scent of Oranges

Bella

A NOVEL

An ordinary cat with an extraordinary gift

JOAN ZAWATZKY

First published in Australia in 2018 by
VeritaxBooks. Victoria, Australia

Website: www.placeofbooks.com

Typeset by BookPOD

ISBN: 978-0-9945532-3-2
eISBN: 978-0-9945532-4-9

Acknowledgements

This book about cats is the result of my admiration, fascination and love for these small, furry animals that were part of my early childhood and my adult life. Writing this book has brought me great joy. I can only hope that readers will find pleasure in reading the story about the closeness and understanding between myself, and my present cat, Tansy. It is to her, and my therapy cat Zoe, now passed, that I owe my thanks for their cuddles and inspiration.

I wish to express my thanks to my husband Hymie for all his support, and to my cat-loving friends who encouraged me to write this book. Thanks to Sylvie and Michael Blair of BookPOD for their publishing expertise, cover design and marketing suggestions.

Summer

'Where are you Precious? Pre...cious!'
I pretend not to hear Karen calling, as I toast in a sunspot behind the curtain. I am too comfortable to move. Perhaps she will give up calling soon. Footsteps! She is looking for me. I will curl up and shift to a warmer spot where she won't see me.

'Breakfast, Treasure!'

She is trying to tempt me out, but she can wait.

I stretch, roll and dig my claws into the soft carpet. The sun has shifted and I give in, slowly answering her call.

'So, there you are, Sweetie!' She says.

Karen is my human owner, a counsellor, who helps unhappy children and teenagers, and visits sick people in hospitals. She works from home in the front room of my house.

She has put me to work as her *Therapy Cat.* While she talks and listens to upset and stressed Humans, my job is to give them my healing love. Cuddles and the positive vibrations of my soothing purrs help them to relax and feel better.

I am paid with heaps of love, cuddles, food, and my accommodation. It is a good arrangement and I am certainly not bored. I have heard her say that I am an ideal cat for the job, with my easy-going temperament, and because I have experienced sadness. She says too, that I am a special cat, naturally affectionate, gentle and aware intuitively when, and how to help.

All of this is true, and I am good at my job.

I like children. They pat and hug me, but sometimes, in the same way as naughty kittens, they make loud noises, pull, or push me. I don't bite or scratch, but if they hurt me, I leave in a hurry.

Though many adult Humans are lovable, many confuse me. They can be unpredictable, illogical creatures with unusual ideas. I have observed that the stressed and unhappy Humans that visit Karen crave care and attention. As most cats, I am independent and a loner, and I have trouble understanding their needs, but I try my best to help with a caring touch of my paw, or a rub.

I realise that Humans have many limitations. They are severely restricted in their movement and are clumsy. They can run, but not as fast as cats. They cannot jump or stretch like us either. Their hearing is extremely poor, and it is sad that they miss so many sounds. I do not know what to say about their sense of smell and taste, other than it is shocking. No wonder, they eat a lot of vegetable food that smells and tastes dreadful.

Karen is an exceptional Human. I trust her completely. My special feeling for Karen, that other cats may be lucky enough to have for their owners, I call Cat Love. I honour her by treating her like a cat, and she appreciates that. There are times, when she is even in touch with what I am experiencing, and walks in my paw steps. Incredible! Sometimes I disobey her to claim my independence, but that does not change my affection for her, or the many times I try to please her in return for the care she has shown me. Of course, she misses many of the subtleties of Cat Communication, and like most Humans, she talks too much.

In spite of her human shortcomings, Karen shines at her work. Her skills encourage me to try harder to assist the Humans I help. If only I could tell her how much I value her depth of understanding – the way she knows what they feel, and how they suffer. Her patience with their long stories, embellished with minute detail constantly amazes me. She *listens intently while my tail quivers with boredom. Most striking, is her ability to clarify human problems and to suggest practical ways of approaching troublesome issues. I learn from her each day, as she learns from me.*

Karen and Tony share the house, but I am most decidedly Karen's cat. He tolerates me and we have a deal. I keep my distance from him, and he puts up with me. Occasionally, when we pass each other, he says "good kitty." I have learned not to look at him, rub against him, or sit on him. It seems to be the best way of handling him. Perhaps eventually our relationship will be warmer. He adores Karen and wants to please her, and as far as I am concerned that is positive.

I believe that there has to be a decent Human inside him, and I am rarely wrong with my intuition.

When I was only a few weeks old, and my eyesight and hearing were just sharpening, Karen rescued me and cared for me.

I will thank her forever.

I was the smallest kitten in mama's litter, and the last one left with her. Humans stole my two sisters and three brothers. One day, a rough hand grabbed me, snatching me away from suckling with mama. The hand shoved me into a bag and removed me from mama's warmth and love. This was the start of my journey away from all I knew. The hand carried me in the bag only a short distance, then it threw me forcefully. I landed with a thump that stunned me at first. My head hurt and I struggled to breathe. Gradually, I managed to wriggle out of the bag and found I was in wet, putrid slime. My tiny paws battled to gain a foothold. Weak and afraid, I called out, *mew, mew.* No one stopped or heard me, apart from a creature I later knew to be a dog. It began to nudge and sniff me. As it started to growl, I heard a human voice. It was Karen's voice. I do not even want to think of what the dog would've, could've done to me if she hadn't been walking past and heard my desperate call. She yelled at the dog and hit it with a stick until it ran away. Then she scooped me into her arms and wrapped me in her warm jumper.

As she carried me home with her, she talked to me in a calm, soothing voice. 'Poor little darling, dumped in the park near the garbage cans. What sort of awful person does a dreadful thing like that? But don't worry, you are safe with me.'

I trusted her then, and later. Even in the toughest of times I knew that she would be there for me. From that moment, my life changed, my path was set. I do not believe in coincidences. I was meant to survive and be found by Karen.

I remember it all, even though I was so little. We cats have incredible long-term memories.

'We're home and safe, Little One,' she said, as she carried me inside.

In the area she called the kitchen, she gave me water and sliced chicken. Then she cleaned me gently with a cloth, stroking me so tenderly, that I felt as if mama was licking me.

To keep me warm, she placed me on a blanket in a small box.

'Somewhere to sleep, Little One. This is where you can pee and poo,' she said, pointing to the litterbox.

Just as well, mama began to teach me to go to the litterbox before I was taken from her.

'I'll be back soon,' she said softly.

I was exhausted and slept. When she returned, she had special kitten food for me. I ate and drank hungrily. While I slept, she hovered over me.

A new, loud voice broke my comfort. It was Tony, the other Human in the house. 'What's going on? Where's this kitten from?' He demanded.

Karen explained to him how she had found me, and that she wanted to keep me.

'Why keep her, just a ginger Tabby? I'd prefer to have a dog.'

Immediately I knew a lot about Tony – a Dog Human, an obedient follower, and not very caring either. How could I trust him? There I was a defenceless kitten, almost killed by a dog, struggling to survive – and he preferred dogs!

'You know I love cats, and I'm keeping her,' she replied decisively. 'Since our darling Samantha died, I've longed for another cat. Anyway, I think she's a beauty. Buy a dog later.'

I realised how strong she was. She would have what she wanted, even if it meant standing up to him.

To keep her happy, Tony finally agreed.

At first, Karen called me Annabella. She liked the name, but it was too long and it did not appeal to me. So, when she called me by that name I ignored her. Later, when she began to call me Bella, I came running to her. I liked being called Bella. It means beautiful, and from what I could see in the big bedroom mirror, it suited me. She has other names for me too, according to her mood. I am her "Good Girl", "Treasure", "Precious", "Beautiful" or "Sweetie". If she is not pleased with me, she calls me "Naughty Cat." One of her favourite words is "No," and she says it loudly and crossly.

I do not worry too much about negatives. I am a positive creature, and explain life in my world, Catland, with Cat Logic and Cat Intuition.

One morning, Karen grabbed me and put me into a carry box. We went on a bumpy ride in the car.

'I'm taking you to the vet. Don't be afraid, Little One, he won't hurt you,' she said reassuringly.

Her kind words did not help. The vet had the smell of many different animals on his white coat. His huge hands prodded me from my head to the tip of my tail. He held me firmly, placed a small, round, silver object on my body and listened to the inside of me through tubes over his ears. Though I tried to pull away from him, it was useless.

'You have a healthy cat, but I will give her all the vaccinations she needs to ensure that she stays that way,' he said, jabbing me with a needle.

Then it was over. It was not as bad as it seemed initially. I knew that Karen would not allow a Human to purposely hurt or harm me.

Once we were home, Karen gave me food and I forgot about the vet.

For the first few days, I stayed in a room at the back of the house.

I felt safe there, until a barking dog scratching at the fence made me nervous. Somehow, he knew I was there and sounded frustrated that he could not reach me. Karen reassured me and even took me outside in her arms to show me how strong the fence was.

Gradually, she encouraged me to venture into the rest of the house. It seemed huge to me then. With my tail down, ears back and my body close to the floor, I sniffed the carpets and furniture. Another cat's scent was everywhere. I discovered that the cat was Samantha, Karen's previous cat, who had travelled over the rainbow a few months earlier. I wondered if her spirit remained. Samantha had marked the entire house as her territory, and her scent was still powerful. In the big bedroom, I noticed a large framed photograph of a longhaired, pale beauty with proud bearing and a bushy tail. She must've been the once, much – loved Samantha.

As my courage grew, I began the enormous task of marking the carpets, all the corners of the walls and every bit of furniture. The house was mine now, and using all my senses, I made it my territory. As I learned the map of the house, I found some places were more important than others to visit often, or avoid if possible. Essential in my daily life were sleeping areas – couches, sun spots, soft chairs and beds. Anywhere Tony preferred to sit or lie were areas of avoidance. Next off my list, were chairs or spots near a door, or with restricted access or vision. Fortunately, the house is huge with a wide selection of secure, sleep areas.

I established my daily routine in the house to provide me with a sense of safety, confidence and knowledge of my *Cat World*. Following a *Cat Pattern* is not at all boring. I thrive on habit and routine, and intensely dislike having it disrupted. Eating, going to my litterbox, playing indoors and outside, and having a lot of sleep is my preferred pattern. Naturally, Karen and Tony have their routines as well, and I do my best to work around them.

My routine works well. I wake when pink blushes the sky, but I wait until the clock's buzzing noise erupts in the big bedroom before I jump onto Karen's side of the bed, and snuggle next to her. Their waking time is predictable for five days. Once Karen is out of bed, I sit in the kitchen and watch the birds through the window until she arrives to give me breakfast. She feeds me food pebbles before she and Tony eat. I ignore their plans for the day where possible, and have my long and necessary morning sleep.

When Karen stops work for lunch I follow her to the kitchen. She fills my bowl with more pebbles, and often feeds me treats as well. Then I wait for her on the couch and we snuggle up together. Most afternoons, I play outside in my garden, and then catch up on more sleep. After dinner, unless Karen and Tony go out, they relax while watching the colour and sound box, they call the television. This is one of my favourite times of day, as Karen enjoys having me near and I receive a lot of loving strokes and tickles from her.

The afternoons and the two days she calls "the weekend" are not as predictable, but I am fed and loved as usual. She has more time for me then, and petting can be a delight, exceeding all my expectations. Some weekends, Karen cooks large meals and invites family or friends. This is when treats can be especially delicious and plentiful.

Karen is my mother now. I love her and return her affection with eye blinks, rubs and head butts. She belongs to me, but as kind as Karen is, she is Human. Fortunately, she is trainable and I have managed to teach her many of my ways. I am not certain if she realises that her home is mine now, and that I have a great deal of Cat Control of what happens in the house – more than she thinks. I have been contented living with Karen.

I am being generous here, but all considered, she has learned well. I have all I need – affection, tenderness, play and understanding. The food is tasty most of the time, and of course, I love her.

She says I have a high Cat Q. Maybe she means that I am smart, but I know that already. I like to learn each day. Enhancing my knowledge about the Cat Universe is important to me. I enjoy challenges, solving problems, and I constantly wonder about Cat Life.

I say it almost every day: Humans are an unsolved mystery. Though Karen is a smart Human, I doubt she is aware of what a complex and amazing creature I am. She calls me her Tabby Cat, and says that I like to play, and that I am loving and gentle. I am almost certain that she has chosen to forget that cats are not merely the sociable, fluffy, loving creatures she imagines. There is another side to us – our Catness. All cats worth their whiskers have Catness. It is about our independence, cleverness and ability to survive by adapting to most situations.

When I matured, the wild cat inside me reared its head. I felt caged in and longed to be free, to roam the streets, climb tall trees and visit the other houses I spotted from the windows. I changed my mind when tomcats prowled and large dogs barked at me. They terrified me to such an extent that for a while I refused to go outside.

That is when Karen asked Tony to build me a small, but safe side – garden, and to build a secure fence around it. At first, he was reluctant to do anything for me. Perhaps he was still missing Samantha, but to please Karen, he created a magnificent garden for me. If we were on friendlier terms, I would be more loving towards him to thank him for making me such a delightful garden.

Karen hardly mentions Samantha, but I can tell that she still misses her. If she didn't miss a cat who had lived in her house, and had given her years of loyalty and affection, what sort of Human would she be? Whenever Karen passes the large, soft chair in the living room she stops to look at it, remembering that it was once her beloved cat's favourite chair. Samantha's hairs remain entangled in the material.

Was Samantha prettier, kinder, cuddlier, or smarter than me? I will never know, and it niggles. Does Karen love me as much as she loved Samantha? Perhaps Tony misses Samantha so intensely, that he cannot accept another cat in the house.

I tell myself that one cat cannot be compared to another. We are all special.

My memories of my Kittenhood spent growing up with Karen are filled with her tender love and care. I was too young then to appreciate how fortunate I was to be rescued by a kind Human who appreciates cats as much as Karen does.

With a kitten's energy, I raced around the house, tugged at, and bit cushions, climbed onto chairs, tables and beds, to exercise my physical skills and gain strength. When I dug my nails into the furniture instead of the scratching post she bought for me, I learned where not to scratch. I saw a different side of her. She insisted that I had to "learn to behave."

When I "went crazy and acted like an uncontrollable feral cat," as she put it, I received the water treatment. This was a cruel form of punishment with a stream of cold water sprayed directly at me. Karen was an expert at hitting my sensitive bits with the spray, and she knew how much I hated being wet.

I sulked when she curtailed my enjoyment of discovering new things, or my investigation of forbidden cupboards, by locking me into the laundry for "time out". It was punishment for ignoring her demands after several requests. She picked me up, said "naughty cat" several times, and then locked me in the tiny room with soap powder and dirty clothes.

Though my stay in the laundry was brief, I hated every minute of it. Consequently, it did not take me long to learn the basics of obeying her, even when it did not please me. The special treats gained for being "a good girl" made it worthwhile.

Karen played a variety of games with me when I was little, and she still does. I can tell that she enjoys playing as much as I do. We play with long feathers on a stick that tickles and move fast, or pretend, creepy snakes. She throws tiny balls for me to chase and retrieve too.

My favourite game is still Hide and Seek. Karen hides first. Though I can smell and hear her, wherever she is, pretending that I can't find her is an important part of the game. I run through the house calling *meow meow*. Then I pounce on her. She strokes me from head to toe, laughs, and gives me a few tasty, small biscuits. When it is my turn to hide, I make it easy for her to find me, or it would take too much of my time. When at last she spots me, I jump up to her and purr loudly. Biscuits follow then too.

I learned to appreciate Karen the hard way. She is rarely sick, but one morning when I was about eight months old, I heard her complaining. When she tried to stand, she fell back onto the bed. Miserable and in pain, she lay in the darkened room for three days, unaware of me. Tony fed me, but forgot to change my water. I drank from the dripping tap.

Without Karen to look after me, I was lost and afraid. I realised then, how important she was to me, and not only for my food. I loved her more deeply than I imagined.

As I developed into an adult cat, her gentle words helped me to forget the rough hand that threw me next to the garbage bin. I became a confident cat, rarely afraid unless I was threatened. I learned about the bliss of lying next to her, the delightful aroma of her body, the thrill of tummy tickles, and gentle chin rubs. Food was another form of her loving, whether she gave me pebbles, chicken, or divine, fishy treats. *Most of all, I learned that life with her was beneficial in every way.*

One sunny afternoon, I was sitting on Karen's lap after lunch revelling in a tummy rub, when she told me that she had decided I was old enough to become a *Therapy Cat,* or as some called it, an *Emotional Support Cat.*

I looked up at her. A *Therapy Cat?*

'Bella, my sweetie, you will be in your basket in my therapy room while I am talking or listening to sad and worried people. Your job will be to follow your affectionate instincts by comforting them and easing their sadness. Your deep purr and cuddles will be important ways you will help them.'

I understood, or I thought I did.

'You'll be my first *Therapy Cat.* Samantha, the darling, was too nervous with people for that special type of work. You are at ease with them, and they like you. I am sure that you will be a great *Therapy Cat.'*

She stroked my head and rubbed my cheeks. I glowed with delight and pride. It is important for a cat to feel useful and to have purpose.

'One thing, Treasure...you will need a certificate from the vet before you can work with me.'

Fat Rats! What was a certificate? Whatever it was, it seemed strange that I needed it, and from the vet, before I could help Karen with my purr therapy.

Humans have so many rules. Some of their rules like this one seem unnecessary and useless.

She took me on another bumpy ride to the vet. This time, I was not concerned about the visit. We saw the same Human with large hands. When he placed me on the cold table, he was gentle as he examined my small body. I trusted him.

'Any problems with Bella?'

'No she's a delight.'

'Do you feed her raw meat? Some authorities believe that a raw diet spreads bacteria and parasites to people.' He shrugged. 'It doesn't make sense to me. In the wild most of a cat's diet is raw meat.'

'She eats nothing raw.'

'Good. You don't want her blamed for making anyone sick.'

He felt me all over, as he talked. 'Cats don't judge people or ask questions. They are a calming presence. People relax with them. As a person looks into a cat's eyes, a bond between Human and cat is formed. Their purrs are thought to lower a person's heart rate and blood pressure. Being emotionally involved with a cat also helps people to forget the past and themselves, and creates a sense of wellbeing.'

He held me firmly and felt my claws.

'Her claws are too sharp and too long, and could be dangerous. I know that Bella is not aggressive and wouldn't scratch anyone, but the tips of her claws need trimming. Watch how I do it, and be sure to do this every few weeks.'

I didn't like the idea of losing my *Cat Weapons,* my sharp claws, but I had no option. He worked quickly and I felt no pain. My claws were intact. They could still function as they were meant to.

'All done! Bella had all the vaccinations she needs when I last saw her. She is set to work safely with people.' He stroked my head. 'With your easy-going personality, you'll make an excellent *Therapy Cat.*'

He wrote on a piece of paper, gave it to Karen, and we left.

What a thrill. I was now a fully-fledged, certified *Therapy Cat* and ready to start my new job as soon as Karen needed me.

'Come, Sweetie. I need you in the therapy room,' she calls.

'*Meeeeow*! I'm coming!' I answer excitedly.

This is my first experience as a *Therapy Cat.* I run to my new basket in the sunny corner of Karen's room at the front of the house, waiting to do my job. It is a comfortable basket, but a workbasket. It isn't as soft and warm as my sleep basket. After all, I am expected to stay awake during therapy sessions. I promise myself that I will not drop off to sleep unless the sessions become excessively boring.

Perhaps I will find some answers to my questions about Humans.

Two Humans enter the room. A plump, worried looking mother holds the hand of a small, skinny girl. She is trembling like a scared kitten.

'What a beautiful cat,' the girl says, approaching me cautiously.

I'm a little tired of hearing how beautiful I am, but it is true, after all.

'Talk to Bella, she likes children...and she won't hurt you,' Karen says.

The child moves closer and bends over me. I smell her sweetness like new spring grass. She has curly, yellow hair and green, cat-like eyes. She holds out her small hand, waiting for me to approach her. I know what to do. I withdraw my claws, purr loudly, and place my paw in her hand.

I sense that she is a special child, who loves and

respects cats.

'Bella, I had a cat too. His name was Chi,' she whispers to me, as she pats my head. 'I loved him lots and miss him so much. He was very sick and died. I was sad and still miss him...but I'm not allowed to have another cat. Chi's fur made Dad so sick that he couldn't breathe.'

After talking to me and stroking me a few times, she stops trembling.

'Leave the cat now, Mia. Come and sit over here,' the mother insists.

Reluctantly, she leaves me to sit next to her mother. While they all talk, I pretend to be asleep, but I listen and watch. This child is interesting. She moves gracefully – almost like a cat.

The mother looks from Karen to her daughter. 'I don't know what to do. Mia is seven, and being bullied. Children in her class pull her hair and call her nasty names. She is nervous and refuses to go to school. I'm very worried about Mia and hope you can help her.'

Mia begins to cry. 'They're horrid and call me a freak.'

Cats Alive! How dreadful! I remember as a tiny kitten barely able to stand, my bigger, fatter brothers and sisters pushed me away from mama, so that they could have most of the milk. I was hungry all the time. It was awful, but it was a long time ago.

This child's body will grow stronger, but she needs to learn how to become stronger inside, and to stop being so upset. Humans worry too much!

Tears fall like rain from the child's eyes. I go to her, rub my head against her legs, and then put my paw on her knee. I look at her, so that she knows I understand how sad she is. She is too little for me to sit on her lap, but there is space for me next to her on the chair. I jump up close to her and purr loudly. Soon she stops crying.

'What an amazing cat!' The mother says. 'Mia seems to like her.'

'Bella understands,' the child says.

Karen looks at me with her loving look.

This is my first attempt as a Therapy Cat, so I'm pleased Karen is happy with me.

Karen listens as the mother talks again. They talk for ages and Karen asks many questions about Mia. Most of it passes over me, but I hear that Mia is smart for her age, and is talented too. She plays something called a violin.

'If it's okay with you, Mia, I will talk to your teacher about the bullying. I'm sure she will help to stop it. With her support, I hope you'll feel more confident about going back to school,' Karen says.

Mia nods, but still looks unhappy.

Karen takes Mia's hand. 'The first step is to try to be brave, and to go back to school to show the bullies you're not scared of them. Take it slowly, and with your teacher's support you'll feel more confident, I'm sure.'

The mother nods in agreement.

Cats know about bullies. Dominant, aggressive cats are part of Cat Life. We come across bullies constantly. The dominant cats dislike anyone who is different or new in their area, and attack viciously if their territory is crossed.

Mia's teacher may be able to help her, but Mia will have to learn to stand up to the bullies...hiss and growl at them like we do when we are threatened by Cat Bullies. She will have to find a way to keep them in their place, but it will not be easy for her. Though I may seem quiet and friendly, if a strange cat would dare to enter my territory, I would hiss and snarl.

'Please come to see me again in a week, to tell me what's happening at school,' Karen says. 'I promise to keep in touch with your teacher. Together we will sort it out.'

'I hope we will,' the mother says.

Mia looks at her mother, and then gives Karen a half-hearted smile.

I shift around in my basket. I wish Karen would hurry up. I'm starving!

At last, Karen stands.

Mia touches my head. '*Meow, meow* Bella,' she says softly.

The room is empty now, but it smells of Humans. I roll and stretch in the next room, where the air is fresher.

Karen strokes me affectionately. 'You were great with Mia, my sweet Bella. Thank you!'

'Lunch, Bella,' she calls.

I run ahead to the kitchen and see her filling my bowl with the same little pebbles I usually eat for lunch. Reluctantly, I eat the hard bits, while she is perched on a high chair. I smell her food – vegetables, that are not at all tempting. Perhaps there will be something tastier for my dinner.

After lunch, we snuggle up together on the couch like two cats. This is one of the special times of my day.

For a few precious moments, I sense her with me in Catland.

'I love you, Bella, and the children who come to see me will adore you,' she says, as she tickles me in all the right places. I go on a short trip to paradise. When the joyous tickle is over, I rub my cheek against Karen's arm and purr loudly to say, thank you. As she relaxes, I fall asleep in her arms.

While we are together, I am totally hers, filled with Cat Love for her. I think of nothing else but her, and the pleasure of being with her. As soon as we move apart, the spell is broken and I have other thoughts. Sometimes, I wonder why love is like food for Humans. They need such a lot of it – constant refills and reassurance, and it is consumed incredibly fast. Perhaps being so big and having almost no hair on their bodies has something to do with it. We are little and have our fur coats to keep us warm inside.

Rats! Tony is in a bad mood today. He curses and stomps complaining of feeling sick. Soon he begins to sneeze and cough. He puts on his pyjamas, even though it is a hot day. He mutters as he goes to bed, and sleeps for a long time. When he wakes, he is grumpy. He calls loudly for Karen, and asks for hot tea.

'It must be that cat of yours making me sick,' he growls. 'She is on our bed every night. No wonder I am sick. I gave into you when you brought her home and wanted to keep her, but I shouldn't have. Now look at the mess I'm in!' He rubs his eyes and sniffles.

I feel all his negativity directed at me.

My fur stands up on the back of my neck. Insulted, I turn my back on him, pretending he does not exist.

I listen to Karen trying to soothe him. 'I'm sorry you're not feeling well Tony, but it's not Bella's fault. Remember our darling Samantha? Her long hairs were all over our bed. I had to change the linen every few days, but you didn't complain about her.'

'Well get that cat out of here,' he says in his whining voice. 'I don't want her near me when I'm sick.'

'Stay in bed today. I'll bring you a hot drink with lemon and honey, and I'm sure you'll feel better soon,' she says and gives him a hug.

Fat Rotting Rats! I turn around to glare at him, and very slowly leave the room. I will not go near him now. He has upset me dreadfully.

When he recovers and returns to work, we continue to ignore each other.

We cats are sensitive and proud creatures and have excellent memories. We do not forgive those we dislike.

Today my house is bright and sunny and big, black, humming creatures fly around. Trying to catch them is fun, but not easy. They must have many, busy eyes, and see my paw just as it is about to swat them.

Karen is out shopping and I will have a lazy day. The house is mine, and I race down the passages as fast as I can to free myself of built up energy.

Through a side window, I watch the children next door playing with a ball. They bounce and throw their ball, and enjoy themselves. Their dog is running after them yapping.

I have come to the conclusion that dogs have no sense and react to everything.

What stupid, pack animals they are, constantly on the lookout for a leader. Imagine one of those spoilt doggies alone in the wild. They couldn't survive without their pack of dogs and a leader. In the wild, we cats sometimes live in colonies, but we hunt alone, and manage just fine. Dogs have relied on Humans for so many years that they are unable to think for themselves. Dreadful! They follow their owners with idiotic loyalty and even lick them all over. A cat is far too proud and independent for that form of subjugation.

I am about to fall asleep on the big bed, snuggled into Karen's soft pillow with the sweet scent of her hair. It is my favourite sleeping and dreaming spot. Anyone who has watched a sleeping cat's eyelids flicker, or legs twitch while they sleep, will know that we dream.

Sleep is a miracle, and it removes me from the world to a place of peace broken only by dreams.

I wake refreshed from my dream.

It was a cold night, and I was alone on a high, mountain peak. Cold wind swirled around me, carrying the sounds and scents of animals of the desert. I sniffed the air and surveyed the endless sand and hills of stone beneath me – my territory. Little food was available in winter, which meant that my hunting area had to be wide if I was to eat. After catching and eating a bird, I drank from an almost dry mountain spring.

In the morning, I remained on the mountain where I was safe, and slept until the sun disappeared.

I dream this dream often. It reminds me of who I am – my *Cat Heritage* from many, many moons past.

I lie on the soft bed with no one to push me away, scold, or hurry me. Relaxed after my sleep, I do my washing, just as mama taught me. I wet my paw with my rough tongue and begin with my heaviest fur. My tail needs a thorough tongue clean too. Each claw I pull out with my teeth, lick clean, and wash. Then my soft pink bits require a lot of cleansing, tongue work. My tongue with its tiny barbs does a great cleaning job. Fresh now, I stretch, and roll on the bed to remove any of my dead hairs. Then I jump off, leaving my hairs on the bed, rather than on me.

Cleanliness has always been essential to Cat Life. Removing our scent, allows us to sneak up on our prey and catch it.

I enter the cool, white bathroom. Into the shower I go, pee over the little round thing with holes in it, and watch my yellow liquid run through them. It's all gone. This is the best peeing place in the house. I like the clean, cool feeling here, so I do this often. The best part is that Karen and Tony will not find out.

Now I check my house, my *Cat Territory*, leaving my mark on every corner, on all the carpets and all the furniture.

Distributing my scent is a huge, but important Cat Job. This is my house and it must have my scent.

Tony will freak out when he sees my hairs on the bed and carpets, but I will ignore him. He will no doubt mutter curses about me again, while he uses that buzzing machine, they call a vacuum. Karen is smart to leave the buzzing to him.

When I think of it, I wonder if Tony realises how smart Karen is. She usually gets exactly what she wants with little hugs and kisses. In her own way, she is very much like a cat. But, I have to admit, that he is far cleverer than her with things that need knocking, or fixing.

Before I arrived, he made a tall, indoor tree for Samantha. Well, it is mine now. I enjoy climbing onto the platforms and hiding in the tunnels. The carpet material around it is perfect for exercising my paws and leaving my scent.

I am about to go through the cat door into my garden to play, when I hear Karen's voice. 'Bella, Bella, Treasure, I need you now!'

There is an urgent tone in her voice. Though I usually take my time to respond, I follow her immediately to the therapy room.

I settle in my basket, as she hurriedly tidies her desk. A lean, sixteen-year-old in denim jeans and a T-shirt walks hesitantly into the room.

I am learning more about age in Humans.

He looks at Karen, at me, and then his glance sweeps around the room. He is like a cat checking his territory.

'Hi,' he says, tentatively, 'I'm Aron...my doctor sent me.'

Karen smiles at him and says, 'I have the letter from Dr Pierce, Aron. Please make yourself comfortable.'

'Hello Little One,' he says to me in his sad, but kind voice. I purr as he pats my head.

'My cat's name is Bella,' Karen adds.

He sits next to me on the carpet with his legs crossed. I sense the darkness around him and his unhappiness.

'How can I help you, Aron?' Karen asks.

I watch him scratch the soft fur on his face and his attempt to hold back tears. He does not speak yet. To comfort him, I jump into his lap. He runs his fingers through my fur and sighs. As I snuggle up to him, I notice that he smells different to Karen and most other Humans – a strange, vegetable smell, nothing like the scented catnip Karen plants in my garden.

Karen waits patiently for him to speak.

At last, his words tumble out. 'Things aren't working out for me.'

I listen, and try to understand why he is unhappy.

'My dad is an engineer working on rail projects. Due to dad's work, we've moved home six times and I've been to four different schools.' Aron wipes away his tears with the back of his hand. 'I'm just beginning to catch up with a class and find a few mates when dad says we have to move again.' He sighs again. 'It's tough and I'm not handling it. Lately I've been smoking a lot of grass.'

It must be difficult to keep moving home. I wouldn't like it either. Having a place of my own is extremely important, but we cats are survivors and adapt.

It is sad that so many of the young Humans who come to see Karen have a sick spirit. When we cats are sick or sad we hide in dark places until we feel better, and then bounce back.

I wonder what grass is. What a pity that Humans don't like catnip.

He keeps stroking my coat, as he stares out of the window before speaking again. 'Things aren't going well at home. My parents have been yelling at each other for months. Mum bursts in tears, and then dad bangs the door and walks away. They can't sort it out, so they've decided to split.' He stares at the carpet while continuing to stroke me almost automatically. 'A split may work out better for them, but it won't be easy for me. To make things worse, they've asked me to choose which parent I want to live with.'

'That's a tough one and not fair,' Karen says.

'The truth is, I don't want to live with either of them. I'd prefer to stay with my sister and brother-in-law in the city. They've said that they would be happy to have me...that is, with my parent's permission.'

'As hard as it is, you'll have to talk to your parents. Being honest with them will be best for everyone in the long run,' Karen says.

'I've had enough, and I don't want to be involved with my parent's problems any longer. I'm sixteen and it's time I had a choice.'

'But, they are your parents, and they care about you. If you move in with your sister, they will want to know details – costs, if you're going school or looking for a job, and about your safety...and that's how it should be.'

'I guess you're right.'

'It may not be that easy. So, if you have difficulties sorting it all out you're welcome to come to see me again. Or, perhaps ask your parents to come along, and we can have a family session...discuss things together.'

Sad Cats! Aron is still a kitten inside, too young to make such difficult decisions. He needs more help. We cats live with our mothers until we are ready to leave. Mostly we don't even know our fathers.

He strokes my head again. 'Thanks Karen. I'll have to see

how things work out. I'll probably be back to you again, with or without my parents.'

He pats the top of my head and says, 'Bye, Bella,' and leaves.

I like my job. It is interesting, and if I help to calm troubled Humans, at least my life has purpose.

It is night when I pass the velvet armchair, I call Samantha's chair. Out of respect, I do not try to rub away what is left of her scent. Though she still visits her old territory and watches Karen, it is time she left. This is my house now.

Tony adored her, I can tell. When Karen mentions her name, his face goes soft, his eyes misty. I am sorry that I have taken his beloved cat's place.

There's nothing I can do to change Cat Fate!

Underneath Tony is sensitive and caring, but he conceals it. Though Karen is gentle, she is far tougher than him...and she makes all the important decisions.

I wake from a sleep feeling peckish, and go to my bowl in the kitchen. In the moonlight, I notice a slight movement on Samantha's chair. A pale, shadowy image of a cat stands tall and proud. Only her eyes glow. I remain silent and motionless, aware that she is watching me. She does not move either. There were moments while I was with Karen, that I sensed Samantha's spirit hovering. Now that she is here, I am not afraid of her presence. She is doing what most cats who were attached to their territory and owner do. She is checking her territory before handing it to me. Perhaps she was staying close to Karen because she loved her, and could not leave her. Or, she is ensuring that I care enough about Karen, and that I am treating her well. She may even be warning me to look after her.

She knows that when we give our love to a Human, it is forever.

I don't know how long we are together in the pale light. Patiently, I stay with Samantha until she leaves. A slight breeze, a curtain ruffles, and she is gone. I wonder if I will see her again.

I am in the kitchen searching the floor and bench tops for bits of spilt breakfast. Tony and Karen are messy eaters. I find a slither of delicious meat. Then I go to my food bowl. Karen has filled my bowl with new, disgusting, food pebbles. I spit them out all over the kitchen floor and make a pile of yellow vomit on the carpet.

That will show her! The new food is revolting!

Meeyuk! I refuse to eat inferior or foul tasting food.

Later Karen sees the food on the floor...and my vomit. She sighs deeply and stares me, but she does not shout at me.

That's a positive about Karen. She isn't angry if I vomit.

'What's wrong Bella? Either you hate the food or you're sick,' she says.

I run and jump to show her that I am well. Instead, I sit and stare fixedly at the cupboard, where she keeps the tasty dry food. Then I move to my empty food bowl and wait. She nods.`

She has received the message.

'Oh, so you're being a princess again! You are telling me that you hate the cheaper brand of food I bought you and it makes you feel sick. I should've known that you only like the best.'

Absolutely!

She laughs, goes to the cupboard and moves things about inside it.

'You'll like these, I'm sure,' she says, pouring new larger pebbles into my bowl.

My nose quivers at the fishy smell. I want to rush to try the food, but I hold back, not allowing her to think I am too keen. Now that's what I call food! I only hope she doesn't try to give me the cheaper brand again.

Computers must be very important to Humans.

Karen is working on her computer again. If she isn't listening to people's troubles, she is sending letters on her computer. Then there are all the phone calls she makes too. When she completes her work, she goes to the kitchen for a quick lunch. She has only a brief Catnap after lunch, and I am usually next to her while she rests. Tony is on his computer a great deal too – after work until dinnertime, and on the weekends. Some evenings they are both too tired to talk or cuddle on the couch.

I hope that they will have a kitten soon, but I think they are too tired to make one.

While Karen is busy in her office, I sleep.

I dream of handsome, male cats that parade past my garden fence. I call out, flirting with them, and they try to look big and bold to attract my attention. They call to me, but I ignore them. I am sad that I can no longer have kittens.

I wake and stretch.

Fat Rats! Karen is still busy on the computer.

Meeeow, meewow. Look at me, notice me, I purr loudly and touch her leg with my paw.

'Hello, Treasure,' she says in a distracted voice.

Not good enough!

I climb onto her desk, push her pens about and walk over her papers. Then I kick tiny silver things onto the floor to remind her that I am here. I nudge her arm until she makes an error.

'Stop it, Bella! Get down!' She says in a loud, cross voice.

I kick her papers onto the floor before climbing down. Once I am in my basket I turn my back on her.

She can try to ignore me, but it never works. She ought to know that by now.

At last, she finishes her work. 'What's with you today, Sweetheart? You know how much I love you.'

I turn about just enough to see her, ignore her, and find a cool spot under the fan.

My fur coat feels heavy and my paws are sweating.

Our paws sweat when we are hot or scared, but at least we don't stink like Humans when they sweat.

'Wake up, Bella...lunch!' She calls.

Talk of food usually moves me, and she knows it.

After I've eaten she calls me again. 'Come, Bella, my treasure, I have something special for you to watch. I hope you will enjoy it.'

I follow Karen to her computer.

She fiddles with it and then pats her lap. 'Come sit.'

I jump up and she points to the screen. I see two adult cats and listen. They are talking to each other, *Pree, prup, pree prup.* It is as if I am watching them through a window. They rub and lick each other, and continue their chat. I try to join in and talk to them, but they can't hear me. Watching them talking makes me feel lonely. I want a friend to chat with too. Karen makes them talk again and again, and strokes my head as I purr. I rub Karen's hand with thanks, and jump down.

I enjoyed watching them. I hope to watch them chatting again soon.

'Don't leave, Precious, I'm expecting Emma in a few minutes, and I need you,' she calls.

I go to my basket in the therapy room and wait. Emma arrives with her mother. I notice that Emma is a few years older than Aron, and looks unhappy. She is dressed in a black dress that clings to her curvy body. After Emma greets Karen, she sits on the edge of her chair looking uncomfortable.

I sniff her from my basket. She hasn't washed for a while.

'How are you?' Karen asks.

Emma looks down and shrugs. 'Fat and ugly!'

I'm feline, and thank goodness for that. Whether I am fat or thin is of no concern to me. Being well-fed and healthy is important to me and most cats. She looks fine when I compare her to some of the skinny Humans who come here. A little fat is useful in times when no food is available. But, one key point, personal hygiene and cleanliness is of prime importance, and I wash regularly.

Emma's mother looks concerned. 'Emma is hardly eating and she hasn't slept for nights. She has been too weak to attend school.'

Emma looks down. Her face is dark, her body tense and her hands clenched. 'Okay, Mum, that's enough!'

She's angry. If she were a cat her ears would be back and her tail swishing.

'I think it might be best for Emma to talk to me alone,' Karen tells Emma's mother. 'If you like, you can wait for her in the sitting-room.'

'I prefer to wait in the car!' Her mother says, looking upset as she leaves.

Emma stretches. 'Phew! She just doesn't get it!'

'Well, she's gone now. Tell me what's happening?' Karen asks.

'I haven't told her yet that I've broken up with my boyfriend, Steve. She makes such a fuss over things. Steve and I were together at the start of high school.'

'So, why did you break up with him?'

'He found someone else...a girl he liked better. I've seen her picture. She is thin and pretty...and I'm a fat, ugly lump. No wonder he dumped me.'

'I'm sorry that you've broken up,' Karen replies. 'Guys his age can be like cats and roam.'

I doubt that Emma is fat and ugly, but how can I tell? Most importantly, she is miserable and dislikes herself. It's a pity she won't confide in her mother.

She looks down and tells Karen that someone made nasty remarks about her on Facebook. Tears dribble down her face, and Karen passes her tissues.

I am sorry that Emma is unhappy, but I won't go to her. She hasn't acknowledged me. Perhaps she doesn't like cats, and that's her choice. A pity that she is upset about her boyfriend, but there are so many males out there. We female cats don't need to stay with one for long.

Karen and Emma talk for so long that I fall asleep. When I wake, they are still talking about Facebook, whatever that is. Emma has stopped crying. She promises to do the homework Karen has given her to help her change negative feelings she has about herself.

I hope that whatever Karen suggests will help Emma.

As she is about to leave, Karen says, 'Try to talk to your mum. She's worried about you...and she probably understands more than you think. She was young too.'

I can't understand why Humans often feel negative about themselves. So many who come to Karen for help dislike themselves. We are proud of our Catness. We put ourselves first and like ourselves, or we will not survive. It is important for us to worry about things like guarding our territory, eating sufficient and keeping safe.

Karen is on the phone again. She is busy constantly apart from a few breaks.

I leave her and forget about the many distressed young Humans. I go through the special door into my garden. It is large enough for a long run. Part of my garden is grassy with flowers that I have nibbled. It has many shrubs, half a tree, and a tall scratch pole. They cut off the top layers of the tree to make it safe, so I wouldn't be able to climb too high, fall or have trouble climbing down. At the back of the garden next to the wall, is a covered place where I can rest and sleep in the heat, or find protection from wind and rain. My poo and pee area is nearby. When Tony erected the high fence around my garden, he ensured that dogs and tomcats could not scale it to attack me. Its height also prevents me from escaping. He cleverly added a locked gate for Humans to enter.

I am grateful to him for creating my safe, beautiful garden. If loud, barking dogs come up to the fence, they are no longer a problem. I jump up, slip my claws through the wire, and scratch them. It does the trick. He planted many flowers and shrubs – far more than necessary. Perhaps he was trying to please Karen. Through the fence wire, I am able to chat to my friends, Brown Cat and Little Grey. There is always a lot to say, but we want to play together. I hope that Karen will open the fence gate to let them in soon.

At times like this, when the bushes are showing off their colourful flowers, many birds fly into my garden.

Cats Alive! Of course, I try to chase birds and other small outdoor creatures. Cats hunt and always have. It is a natural part of our lives, though Humans have trouble accepting it. We are small, but powerful predators. Our mothers teach us to pounce, chase and hunt from an early age. It upsets me that I've had no luck at all with catching birds. Karen interfered with nature by putting a little bell on my collar. She insists on it being there, and as much as I shake my head and meow for her to remove it, she refuses. Just when a bird is near enough for me to pounce, the silly bell tinkles to warn the bird, and it flies off. It is unfair, and extremely frustrating! I am sure that the birds laugh at me. Just imagine, the disgrace – a cat that can't even catch a bird!

I head for the trunk of the half-tree and scratch again and again until I have released my frustration about hunting for birds that will never be.

The hot weather makes me lazy. I am relaxing for a few moments and then I will start my exercise circuit. I shoot up the half-tree to the top, and then race around the rest of my garden three times. But first, a sniff of the special grass, Catnip, that Karen plants for me. Breathing it, or rubbing the leaves on my body, puts me in a happy mood for the day.

What is that! I notice something moving... close... very slowly. Ha! It's a lizard! Gotcha! Snap its head off! A present for Karen! I carry it inside carefully and drop it at her feet. I close my eyes and say 'I love you.'

Karen is not as pleased as I had hoped.

She bends to stroke my head. 'Thank you, Bella, my treasure. I know that this is a special gift. You're treating me like a Cat Mama, and showing me how well you can hunt for your food.' She smiles and pats my head again. 'Sorry, my sweetie,' she says, as she wraps the lizard in paper and throws it into the garbage bin.

Karen tries to cover her yawns this morning. After lunch, she lies on the couch for a nap. She is so tired that she sleeps until the doorbell rings it's loud song. She jumps up, smooths her hair, puts her clothes in place, and rushes to open the door.

She says she doesn't need me all afternoon. Even though she is busy, she is seeing Humans who dislike cats.

There are lots of them – Humans who dislike animals or are dog lovers.

When she has finished her work, she is too tired to cook dinner.

Cat Alert! Karen is working too hard and too long, and doing too many different things at once. She doesn't take enough time for herself.

Humans like cats become stressed and even sick, if they do too much. We avoid creating our own stresses – an important rule of Catness. Dogs, nasty Humans, cold weather and lack of food create more than enough stress in our lives. We grab every opportunity to relax and sleep to fortify our bodies and remain in top condition.

She phones Tony to bring dinner and leaves food for me. Then, she goes to her room, and falls asleep on the big bed with me lying next to her. When Tony brings her a plate of food, she wakes. They have a long conversation about her tiredness. Finally Karen agrees that she is working too hard, taking hardly any breaks, and doing no exercise.

A few days later, a huge package arrives. When she opens it, I recognise a bicycle. I watch Humans riding bicycles through the front window. Later, when Tony finds a place for it, I realise that it is a different sort of bicycle, meant to stand still. It has bicycle wheels, but it stands on a base that makes it stationary. Tony fiddles with it until he is satisfied that it is stable. Then he sits on it and moves the pedals. The wheels whir around fast until Tony stops. He is puffing and panting.

'It is a top exercise bike,' he says to Karen. 'It will help us both to keep fit.'

Karen tries it out, but cannot manage to make the wheels turn as fast as Tony does.

'I've had enough,' she says, after a few minutes. It will take me ages to build up my fitness.'

'You need to take a morning break and do some exercise or you'll be sick,' Tony says, giving Karen a hug. 'I do quite a lot of walking to and from the bus stop to work, but you work at home and do very little walking.'

'You're spot on! I'm going to take a morning coffee break and a few extra minutes on the exercise bike every day.'

I am with Karen in the therapy room, when she looks at her watch. 'Time for a break and exercise,' she says.

I follow her to the side of the television room, where Tony has put the exercise bicycle. It is time for my exercise too. I feel a spurt of energy needing release and race around the house until I am tired. At the same time, Karen is riding her bike.

Keeping fit is another aspect of Catness. Being strong enough to chase prey or run from predators if they attack is essential.

The wheels of Karen's bike stop turning. She is breathing hard and falls onto the couch. Then, while I lap water, she goes to the kitchen to make herself a cup of tea. I sit next to her and rest, as she slowly drinks her tea.

There is a part of me, deep beneath my furry coat, that knows it is a weird idea, but I hope that my Karen is learning Catness.

Mid-Summer

The early sun greets me, filtering through the curtains and making bright spots on the floor. As I wait for Karen to open the door to my garden, I chase the flitting light across the room.

At last, I hear her unlocking the door. I have fun running and hiding behind bushes and pouncing at rocks. Then I chase my tail, imagining it is a mouse. When the heat drives me inside, I rush to the coolest part of the house, directly under the big blower. My fur coat is thick, hot and heavy. Right now, I would like to be as hairless as a Human.

Karen tries to "cool me down" by wiping me with a wet towel, but water treatment of any kind is abhorrent, so I run from her.

It is Friday, and Karen is in the hot kitchen baking for the weekend. She gives me sweet, soft bits of cake. *Yumow!* She says I am weird because cats rarely like cake, and that most cats do not have taste buds for sweet things.

When she leaves to go shopping, the cakes sit partly covered to cool on the benchtop. I circle them. What a huge temptation! One swoop of my paw could snap off a chunk of deliciousness, but this once, I exercise restraint and eat my boring pebbles.

She returns carrying a large box. I watch and wait as she places it on the floor.

'Something new for you to play with. I know you like boxes.'

I sniff the outside of the box and chew a bit. It tastes awful, and smells of food and dust. I jump inside. It's dark, but safe, and somewhere to roll around and play. No one can sneak up on me, and I can see everything from here. I scratch the inside and outside of the box to mark it as mine.

Scratching is an amazingly satisfying activity and always a release of any built up tension.

Later, I sleep in the box and have a magnificent dream.

It is night in the desert, and I am alert. The cool night is my hunting time. During the day, the sun burns my nose, so I seek cover and sleep.

Hungrily, I look out from my mountaintop territory for food. No mice or lizards up here. If I want to eat tonight, I will have to climb down the mountain. In the moonlight, I use the pads on my feet and my claws to grip small plants between the craggy rocks, to make my descent. At the foot of the mountain, grass is sparse. There are a few trees and a muddy steam. Guardedly, I check for predators – foxes, wolves and owls. I am safe and I drink. I catch one lizard and then another. After scraping away their tough skin with my claws, I eat their flesh. Satisfied, I check the territory again.

In the darkness I see a bright ball of light, hotter than sunlight. Plumes of grey surge into the sky. I move towards it slowly, prepared to hide or run if threatened. Humans are talking, and I smell charred wood and food.

One calls me. Ssk, ssk cat!

I am afraid, as I know little about these Humans.

Meow, meow, I reply.

He calls again, holding out some cooked meat for me that smells inviting. I edge closer and grab the meat.

I am about to eat the meat when Karen's voice wakes me and interrupts my dream.

'Bella, my precious, something special for you. Soft meat that you like.'

She leaves a few pieces of cooked meat in my bowl. I jump out of my box to eat it. It is gone in seconds.

'Bella...work!' Karen calls.

Half-heartedly, I follow her. I would prefer to go back to sleep and follow my dream.

A loud knock on the door. A tall, agitated mother holding the hand of child in tears, enter the room. The child looks as fragile as a petal in the wind.

'How can I help?' Karen asks, motioning them to chairs.

The mother's words pour out in a jumble. 'Jeremy is four...and hasn't stopped crying since he heard that his big brother Laurie is leaving home to live with a group of his university friends. He has an older sister, but he adores Laurie and is very upset.'

Little Jeremy sits on his mother's lap, sobbing as he clings to her.

My ears are erect, as I try to catch everything that is said. I wonder why the frightened little, kitten boy is crying so much.

Tears fill the mother's eyes. 'My husband and I have separated, and with Laurie leaving as well, it is too much for Jeremy to handle. I hope you can help.'

Cats Alive! The poor little Human. No wonder he's upset, and his mother doesn't know what to do.

'Arguments and the tense atmosphere in the house before we separated upset the children and Jeremy is the worst affected. I wish we had handled things differently.' She sighs and wipes her eyes with her hand. 'I'm worried. In the last month he's been talking "baby talk" again, clinging to me and sucking his thumb.'

Karen nods. 'When parents separate it can upset children more than people think, and they can return to childish behaviour, but it will pass when he feels more secure.'

So many parents who bring their children to see Karen have broken relationships and their children suffer. At least we stay with our mothers and our other family as long as we can. Our fathers are not worth worrying about. Human males have trouble settling down too, it seems.

Jeremy begins to cry again and Karen smiles at him. 'While I chat to your mum, Jeremy, you can sit with Bella. She likes children.'

'Hello Bella,' he says, as he frees himself from his mother. In seconds, he is on the carpet next to me. I purr, and he allows me to put my head on his tiny leg. I move closer, touch him with my paw and he stops crying.

'You're such a pretty kitty,' he says, as he pats me all over.

'You can tell Bella why you've been upset today, Jeremy. She'll understand,' Karen says to him.

He touches my head and whispers. 'Everyone I love goes away and I'm scared. It's my fault that mum and dad aren't going to live together anymore... and that Laurie has gone too.'

He snuggles closer as I rub my cheek against his tiny hand, wet from his tears.

'Both your parents love you, Jeremy. It isn't your fault that they aren't living together, or that Laurie has left home and is staying with his friends,' Karen says, and then adds more comforting words.

While his mother talks to Karen, he continues to stroke me.

Then Karen asks Jeremy how often he sees his dad.

'Dad comes to see me late after work, but most times I'm already sleeping...and mum won't let him wake me.'

'It's a pity you miss seeing him when he comes, but do you see him other times?'

'I go to his house every Saturday and sleep over.'

He bursts into tears again.

His mother throws up her hands and shrugs. 'Maybe changing houses every weekend is upsetting Jeremy.'

Sad Cats! Jeremy is like a lost kitten who has been hurt.

He needs so much love and care – and being pushed from one house to another isn't doing him any good. I rub against him, while purring loudly for him. I am trying to tell him that I care about him and that I want him to feel happy again.

'Jeremy, I can tell that Bella is sad that you are upset,' Karen says. 'We all want you to feel happy again. So, I will talk to your dad...and between all of us we'll make certain that you'll be happier soon.'

Karen asks Jeremy's mother to tell his father that she would like to talk to him about Jeremy as soon as possible.

By the time they leave, Jeremy has stopped crying but he still looks upset.

Meow, meow I cry to Karen, touch her leg with my paw, and then go to the spot on the carpet where Jeremy was sitting.

'Bella, my treasure, I think you are trying to tell me that you are worried about Jeremy. He is going through a tough time and feels alone. He needs lots of loving from both his parents. I hope his father will help.' She pats my head. 'You were great with him and helped him to feel wanted. He left much calmer. Thanks Bella, you amazing cat!'

I jump onto Karen's lap and purr loudly for her.

At last, she puts her papers and her small hand phone away, and turns off the computer. She stretches and smiles.

'Work is over for the weekend.'

Later, Tony arrives with flowers and chocolates for Karen. He carries in brown, small bottles for himself. They hug and kiss. Watching them together makes me feel good. The atmosphere in the house is calm. I like to watch them chat, for their eyes to connect and then their lips to meet in a kiss.

They drink dark liquid and open the box of chocolates. Karen eats many, but Tony only a few. Life at home is so pleasurable.

The flowers are fun to play with. I bite off some of the petals and they fall on the floor, but I avoid the chocolates. I ate a bit of chocolate once and vomited on Karen's soft bedroom carpet. I could tell she was upset, but she wasn't angry with me. All she said was, 'No more chocolate for you...ever again!' Then she washed the carpet until it was clean.

I am in my garden when I hear a swishing sound above me. I look up, and all I see is a blob circling. Then, a birdlike creature as big as me, lands on the grass. It stares at me without any sign of fear or aggression.

Quark, quark, it says.

It has white feathers, a spotted breast, a dark head and beak, and short, strange feet. I haven't seen a bird anything like it before. Why has it landed on my territory?

Cat Alert! I approach it slowly and cautiously, head lowered, ears erect, claws out, and pupils dilated. I am ready to pounce if necessary. The creature ignores me, as it picks at seeds and grass.

It says *quark, quark* again.

Not knowing what to do, I answer *meow meow.*

Suddenly, it surprises me by lifting its weird feet and chasing me. As it runs, it flaps its large wings in the strangest way. It appears to be playing with no intention of attack. I turn about and chase it. When I hide, it finds me. I climb the half-tree. It flies up to me and pecks my tail. I haven't had such fun for a long time. When I search for it, it has disappeared. High above, I see a blob flying away.

Karen comes into my garden laughing. 'So, now you're playing with a duck. You are the funniest cat.'

When Karen leaves, I sit on a rock wishing the duck hadn't left so soon. I am lonely with no one to play with and wish I had a friend. I go to the half-tree and scratch the trunk. After several scratches, I am relaxed and go through the cat door to the inside of the house.

Another hot day.

Karen answers her phone. After a brief greeting, her face crumples with concern. 'I'm so sorry,' she says. 'Poor Helena…how can I help?' She listens, and then replies, 'Yes, I can come and see her and bring Bella along, if you think she will help.'

'Bella, we will have to leave soon to visit Helena, an old lady I have known for a long time. She is sick and in pain. Her daughter says that she is a cat lover and hopes that you can help to ease her mother's pain.'

As Karen opens a drawer to take out my harness and lead, the fur on the back of my neck stands up in revolt.

Sssssss I hate the harness! If only she wouldn't make me wear it, and in this heat too. I flick my tail and glare at her. She has to know that I am not at all pleased with these tools of oppression.

'Come on, silly!' She reads the signs of my dissatisfaction and strokes me gently. 'I know how much you dislike wearing the harness, but when we visit sick people we don't have much choice. We have to follow the rules. All cats visiting sick people must wear a harness and lead, but you know that.'

When Karen showed me the harness for the first time, I sniffed it. It had an unpleasant, sour odour.

'We will have to do some training. You need to wear this

when we visit sick people. It will help them to feel safe with you and make you look more professional – a qualified *Cat Therapist*,' she said, patting my head with a laugh.

I like the sound of her laughing. It's like bubbles of water in her throat.

When she put the *thing* on my body and snapped it shut, it was tight and bit into me. I meowed loudly, but she ignored my discomfort. I ran and hid. Then I did my best to bite the torturous thing around my middle, and pull it off, but it was thick and clung to my fur. As hard as I tried, I could not free myself.

'Right Bella,' I'll take it off now and loosen it. Then we'll try again another time until you get used to it,' she said in her firm voice that I disliked.

It took me three weeks to become accustomed to the smell and feel of the harness, though nothing could make me like it. I wore it to please Karen. Just when I thought my training was over, she produced another article of torture – a lead.

'Treasure, now that you're used to the harness, I'd like you to learn to walk with a lead attached to it. You may not like it, but you'll need to wear the harness and lead when we visit people in their homes and in hospitals. Eventually you'll get used to them both and they won't bother you.'

Karen was determined that I would bend to her wishes. Every day she took out the despicable objects, connected them to me, and attempted to make me walk. There were occasions when I was too angry to please her. I lay on the floor, made myself as heavy as possible and refused to move. She was not at all happy with me and pulled on the lead in the hope of moving me. This made the harness even tighter and more uncomfortable. I absolutely hated it.

I made an instant decision. As much as I loved Karen, I would not allow her to do what she liked with me. I cried louder and louder. She did not have to do this awful thing to me. I was a cat after all – a free, wild creature, a hunter, not born to walk with a lead. Leads were for stupid animals like dogs without free spirits or minds of their own. Unlike me, they were happy being controlled. I had seen them through the window going for walks with their owners. They all wore collars and leads.

Well, Karen could forget it!

I let her know how displeased I was with her by turning my back on her, and jumping out of her arms if she tried to pick me up. One day, when she attempted to put the instruments of oppression around me once more, I hissed at her and dug my nails into her flesh. Red oozed out of her and she ran to the bathroom to clean it. She yelled at me, and even threw her shoe at me. It was the first time she had done that. I dodged the shoe, but I realised how much I had upset her.

I love Karen, and I admit that I had taken my rebellion too far, but I had to make a stand.

When she pretended she could not see me and refused to give me my usual treat of chicken for dinner, I knew I was in trouble. Later, I went to her. She watched me move slowly towards her, my tummy close to the ground, my tail down, but she ignored me. As I rubbed her hand with my cheek, I feared she would push me away.

She sighed. 'You have behaved very badly, Bella...like a naughty kitten, but I adore you, and you know it. I'll forgive you this time, but you *will* have to learn to wear the harness and lead.'

For a few days she wore a bandage on her arm. It was a reminder of what I had done to her. When the bandage came off there were three red marks on her arm. I looked at them every day, waiting for them to heal.

I tried not to feel guilty about hurting her, and told myself that it was not my fault. She had pushed me too far and any cat would've reacted like I did.

Anyway, why was this device so important? Humans have the strangest ideas and their priorities are illogical. They become stuck on things and will not let go! Rules ruled her life.

After a week of peace, she continued with her efforts to persuade me to walk with the harness and lead. I refused to give in, that is, until she bribed me with food. When she held out some tuna, I could not resist the seductive, tantalising aroma and I walked towards her. Each day a whiff of tuna or chicken encouraged me to wear the contraptions and walk a little further.

When confronted with my favourite foods I lose my Cat Sense and all my Cat Ethics. I have to admit that I am not proud of being so weak and easily manipulated.

Eventually, I became accustomed to walking with the harness and lead without a bribe of food. Somehow, her affectionate words and extra strokes made it worthwhile.

Just when I thought my training was over, she produced a big box. When she pulled the sides of the box away, a large object emerged.

'I've bought you a lovely, new carry box that is larger than the old one. It should be more spacious, now that you've put on a little weight. I can take you to see people in this.'

I took one look at the new box and my claws clung to the carpet in rebellion. It was big enough for me, but made of foul smelling plastic. Karen opened the door of the box for me, but I had no intention of entering it. I ran from Karen and stayed hidden, slipping out only to go to my litterbox or to eat.

Eventually I conceded to her demands. I had no choice.

After the harness, lead and now the carry box, I hoped she has no more nasty surprises for me.

What a miserable few weeks.

The day is warm as we set out to visit Helena. As usual, I find car travel unpleasant. I am a bit nauseous, but it will go when we stop. I wear the uncomfortable harness and Karen places me in the new carry box. Even though the plastic container has a soft pillow, I am unable to see much through the tiny holes.

I expect that she will clip on the lead when we arrive at Helena's house. All of it is uncomfortable. Just as well the journey is short.

A Human, called Lily, waits for us outside the house. She thanks Karen for coming, and most of all for bringing me. As I am still in the box I cannot see her, but she has a kind, young voice.

'I'll take you to my mother,' she says.

Inside the house, Karen opens the door of my carry box and clips on my lead. I sniff the carpet and walls as we follow Lily down the passage. I can tell that cats lived here at some time in the past. I hear gasping breaths. Lily takes us into a room where an old woman struggling to breath lies in her bed. Her face is pale and puckered, her eyes are closed and her body is tense.

Lily stands close to the bed. 'Mum, your friend Karen and her cat, Bella, are here.'

Helena opens her eyes to greet Karen. Then she rests her attention on me.

'Ah, Bella, you've come.' She opens her arms to invite me to join her on the bed.

At last, Karen removes my lead but not the harness.

I know she is trying to do the right thing, but she does try too hard at times.

'Take that harness off poor Bella. It is unnecessary in here,' Helena says.

I am uncertain about jumping onto Helena's bed. Between fast gasps, Helena pats the blanket. Karen nods and I am on her bed in seconds. I move closer, near enough for her to touch me.

Helena begins to stroke me with a gentle touch. Only Karen has petted me as tenderly. As she touches my pleasure spots – my tummy, neck, cheeks and behind my ears, I purr. She is a Human who knows a lot about cats, and likes us. I nestle near her chest. Her gasps tell me that this is where she needs extra help and healing. My purr deepens. She relaxes and falls asleep with her hand near my head.

Then the strangest thing happens. While Helena sleeps, her gasps for breath ease, and her body relaxes. Though I try to fight my desire to sleep, it overtakes me. When I wake, the room is almost dark and Helena is still asleep. I hear Lily and Karen's voices in a room nearby. I give Helena's hand a rub, and enter the world of sleep once more.

Later, when Lily comes into the room and turns on the light, I open my eyes. Helena is awake now and stretches. Though her breaths are still laboured, they are slower and a little easier.

'How are you?' Lily asks her mother.

'I'm feeling much better.' Helena stokes me tenderly. 'I felt a healing warmth pass through me,' she says. 'It is all due to wonderful Bella. When I was a child we had cats. I believe that the energy in cat's purrs heal.'

Karen says to Lily, 'Recently I read some scientific articles about the healing power of a cat's purr. Whether is true that they can heal with their purrs, is still uncertain. There is insufficient research so far. But, your mother is looking better, Lily, and her breathing has improved. Relaxing with Bella and a good sleep seems to have helped.'

I enjoy the two of them talking about me. Of course we cats are healers. Everyone knows that.

'Thank you, Bella,' Lily says, as she strokes my head. 'I have something for you, and I hope you will like it.'

She places a saucer on the floor. I sniff the mesmerising aroma.

'Go on, enjoy!'

Meowow Wow! Little bits of fish mixed with other morsels.

There are no words to describe the experience of eating this food. Of course I want more, but there is none.

I rub my head against Lily's leg in thanks, and Karen smiles.

As we leave, Karen agrees to visit Helena with me again.

'You did so well, Sweetie,' Karen says during the drive home.

The tenderness in her voice and the knowledge that I helped Helena, compensates for the burden of wearing a harness and being placed in a carry box during the journey home. At least I am doing something useful.

Fat Rat's! My food bowl is empty. I am starving. Where is my food?

Karen has been exceptionally busy today and has forgotten about me. A *Cat Offence!*

She is at her desk working on the computer.

Meow, meow, I say to her.

'I'm busy Bella, let me finish my work.'

Meeeow, meeeow. I try again insistently.

'No, Bella. I told you, I'm busy.'

I jump up and touch her leg, but she brushes me away. I circle the desk several times crying, but she doesn't notice.

'You are a pest, Bella. What do you want?'

I sit at her feet and lift my paw.'

'You must really want something. I haven't seen you do that before.'

She is behaving so stupidly. When she sits in front of the computer she forgets everything, even me.

Her hand phone rings and she answers. This time she is talking to a friend.

Oh no, not more talking!

In desperation, I show her my tongue.

She looks at the time. 'Goodness, I forgot to put food out for you, my precious.'

She lifts me up and kisses my head. 'I'm so sorry, Bella!' Then she walks quickly towards the kitchen. I run ahead and wait outside the food cupboard. At last she fills my bowl and I eat.

She is back at the computer with a pile of papers next to her.

After my meal I go into my garden. I am about to fall asleep under a shady bush, when I hear *quark, quark*. I am alert in seconds.

Happy Cats, the duck is back! It ignores me as it picks at the grass. I try to sneak up to it, but it is smart. It has seen me and flies off to annoy me. Then we play, as it swoops down and then around the bushes. As hard as I try to catch it, I cannot. I give up and rest on the soft grass. It flies up to me, pecks my ear, and then disappears into the blue.

The sun is hiding behind the clouds when I decide to go inside. I am surprised to find Karen on a mat on the floor.

I watch her, as she curls and stretches her body in many positions. I keep watching, flabbergasted. She is stretching like a cat, and I am delighted that she is copying my stretches. She is on her hands and knees, spreads her fingers and looks down towards the floor. Then she breathes out, drops her head, pulls up her tummy, rounds her spine, and tucks in her tailbone. As she breathes in, she slowly returns to a flat- back position.

She notices me watching her and smiles. 'A cat pose,' she says.

When she has completed her routine, she lies on her back and closes her eyes. In bed at night she sleeps on her side, so I know she is not asleep now. She is floating as cats do when they relax.

We grab every opportunity to relax and fortify our bodies in order to remain in top condition. Cats truly know how to stretch for benefit. We stretch to relieve tension and to restore suppleness. I hope that Karen copies more of my Cat Stretches.

I am thrilled. Every day she becomes more like a cat.

I am asleep in the therapy room, on a sunspot under the curtain, when I hear the doorbell sing. Mia, the girl with yellow hair, who was bullied at school, is here with her mother. She sits on the carpet next to me. I am happy to see her and purr loudly.

'Hello, Bella.' Her eyes smile at me, and I smell her sweet freshness. I am pleased she is not crying today. She gives me a cuddle and I purr with joy.

I can tell that this child adores cats.

Karen tells Mia that she talked to her teacher, Mrs Sands. 'Your teacher was horrified that children in your class are bullying you. She will speak to the bullies, and said it won't happen again.'

The mother sighs. 'Well it did happen again – yesterday. Mia was very upset, and now she refuses to go to school.'

Mia moves closer to me on the carpet and whispers to me. 'I'm never going back to school, Bella. Some of the children are still nasty to me.'

Fat, Stinking Rats! Being bullied is dreadful. Poor Mia!

'Did I hear you tell Bella that you're still being bullied?' Karen asks, looking concerned.

Mia clenches her fists and begins to cry. 'I won't go back. I won't. Some of the children still turn their backs on me and say mean things. Mrs. Sands hasn't helped at all.'

Mia's mum leaves her chair and goes to Mia. She touches her hair and kisses her. 'Don't cry my darling...Karen will help.'

'Of course I will,' Karen says.

'I will talk to Mrs Sands again. She needs to know what is happening.' She takes Mia's hand. 'We are going to sort it out together...you, me, Mrs Sands and Bella.'

Mia looks unconvinced.

'Well, I know that Bella doesn't like seeing you upset, so she's going to help us a lot.'

Mia nods, and strokes my head. 'Yes, I know she likes me, and wants me to be happy.'

'Well Mia, what do you think Bella would do if she was bullied by horrible cats that hissed at her?' Karen asks.

'I don't think she would run away...or try to bite them,' Mia says, looking at me. I purr and snuggle closer.

Karen knows exactly what I would do.

'I think Bella would turn her back on them,' Mia says hesitantly. 'That's what my Chi used to do.'

'Yes, she would turn her back on them and be very angry that they are trying to upset her,' Karen says. 'I know that when Bella is cross with me, she turns her back on me and pretends I am not there. She ignores me.'

Mia nods and smiles.

Karen touches Mia's hand. 'It's time to feel cross enough to treat these nasty children as if they don't exist – ignore them completely. Just like Bella would.'

'Okay, I suppose I can go back to school and give it a try,' Mia says reluctantly, as she strokes me.

'Keep imagining you're a cross, proud cat like Bella, and soon the bullies will stop bothering you.'

Mia kisses the top of my head. 'I love you, Bella', she says.

I put my paw in her hand and purr.

Karen is absolutely correct, I wouldn't put up with those bullies in all my Cat Days. Mia ought to be angry if children are bullying her. I would hiss loudly, as well as turn my back on them. Karen is teaching Mia to stand up for herself. She has to learn to fight back, or her life will be a misery. It's all about learning Catness, or in her case, Humanness!

Before they leave, Karen reminds Mia to bring her violin the following week. 'I'm looking forward to hearing you play.'

Cat Work is over for the day. I am in my garden sitting on the top branch of the half- tree. I look into the backyard of the house next door with its ugly dog, and in all the other houses behind and in front of us. There are dogs and cats in the yards.

The cats are sleeping or playing. The dogs must be loved for the Humans to feed and care for them. I am lonely up here, but I am safe. Sometimes Karen opens the gate in the fence to let in one of the cats I like to play with, but mostly she is too busy and forgets.

The sun is starting to rest in the sky. I run around my garden three times, for exercise, before leaving through the special door that leads to the house.

'You're doing your racing spurt,' Karen says with a laugh. 'You've reminded me to ride my bicycle. I haven't done enough exercise today.'

If Tony is in an exceptionally good mood when I pass him as I race around the house, he'll say, 'Hi, there you go, Bella.' Other times he says to Karen, 'That cat of yours is crazy!'

But I'm not crazy! So what if I race around the house. Tony often goes out to play with a ball. Most mornings, I watch him from the front window and see him running along the pavement. Is that crazy? This is my exercise and why shouldn't I do it?

I am tired, but relaxed as I head for the big bed to sleep on Karen's soft cushion. I am almost asleep when something bright and shiny grabs my attention. It is round and has a silver strap. Karen usually wears it on her arm, but today she has left it lying on the small table next to her side of the bed. I had better put it away for her, or she might lose it. There, I have it in my claws. I play with it, by turning it around and biting it. I drop it, pick it up again, and let it dangle until I am bored with it. Then I hide it under the bed, right in the back corner of the carpet where it will be safe.

Later I hear her shouting, 'Where's my watch? What have I done with my watch?'

She hunts everywhere.

Bad Cat Error! I didn't realise that the shiny thing that was next to the bed was a watch...a time thing.

'Did you take my watch and hide it?' She asks me.

Meeeeow, I say, and slip under the bed towards the corner to show her where the watch is. I try to grab it in my paw but it is stuck. I call out a few times and she ignores me.

'What are you doing under the bed, Bella?'

That night, Tony searches for the watch. 'I'll move the bed. It might have fallen. You never know. Ah hah! I've found it, Karen,' he shouts. 'Bella must've hidden it there. She can be a pest,' he growls.

Karen glares at me, but she doesn't want to scold me in front of Tony. I slink away.

I did try my best to protect her possession, but I have to admit that it was fun seeing them search for it. It isn't as if I didn't try to show Karen where it was. She ought to take more notice of what I tell her.

The sun has gone to bed, the dark sky sparkles with lights and the moon is full. Tony is sitting in front of the television drinking from his dark bottles of liquid and relaxing. I avoid him.

I am adjusting to the idea that perhaps he won't ever change and like me.

Meanwhile, Karen is in the kitchen preparing dinner. I stay near her, but not close enough to be under her feet, or she complains that I'm in her way. Like most nights, she throws me bits of food while she's cooking. She fills my bowl with fresh water and opens a tin of wet food for me. I am hungry and eat most of it, but leave a space in case Karen gives me a little of her food while she's eating. The tinned food is boring and tastes the same whether it's fish or chicken.

They sit on high chairs in the kitchen to eat. I sit nearby and wait. Karen calls me in the soft voice she uses especially for me, and puts a little of her food on a small plate for me. I gobble it up and *meow* for more. I am lucky tonight, she puts another bit on my plate.

'You shouldn't feed Bella from the table,' Tony says crossly.

He is a fast, sloppy eater. He doesn't realise that bits of his food drop onto the floor. I grab a bit now.

Later they both sit on the couch to watch television. I watch with them only if there are ball games.

Humans trying to run after balls and catching them is hilarious, and I enjoy it. They are extremely clumsy creatures.

Karen and Tony are hardly talking. He drinks more dark liquid than usual. Instead of tea in a cup, she drinks coloured liquid from a long glass. They usually sit next to each other, laugh at the television and kiss often, but tonight they look tense, sit apart, and argue. She sighs often, complains that he is drinking too much of his dark liquid, and that he has been coming home late. He replies angrily that she is always tired because she sees too many clients. The atmosphere in the room is heavy and stormy. As their voices become louder, I am scared and upset. I run to the other end of the house and hide behind the heavy velvet curtain where I feel safer.

When there is peace between them again, I sit on her lap. Her radiating love warms me all over, as she strokes and tickles me. I snuggle close to her to show her how much I love her.

They begin to yawn. They stop playing with their hand phones, nibbling crispy bits of food and drinking hot stuff, and start the slow human process of going to bed.

All Cats above! It takes ages for them to wash and get ready to sleep. At least tonight, they haven't closed the door to their bedroom. I wait until they are purring in their sleep and jump onto the bed next to Karen. She whispers to me softly.

Tony wakes during the night. He puts on the little light next to his bed. He goes to the bathroom and returns to bed, but he can't sleep and lies awake until morning.

Humans make such a fuss about sleep. For me, falling asleep is easy and I can do it anywhere. After eating, sleeping is my next favourite thing, and I sleep a lot – at least sixteen hours a day. Humans know so little about us.

Why we sleep a lot, is a mystery to Karen. She often laughs at me and calls me Sleepy Cat. She ought to realise that we are most active when the sun has gone to bed, which means we have to catch up on sleep during the day. After breakfast is my best time for a snooze. Possibly, she forgets that even a housecat like me is instinctively a predator, wired over generations to hunt at night. Hunting uses up an enormous amount of energy, and we need reserves, whether we are pouncing on a mouse, or playing with toys. Like Humans, we doze, sleep deeply and dream. When we doze, we position our bodies to spring into action if attacked. I wish I could explain all of this important Cat Information to her.

Today, Jeremy's father comes to talk to Karen.

'Hi, Puss!' He says.

He is tall and lean, with strong muscles for a Human. I pretend to be asleep, while I listen and watch Karen talk to him.

'I am worried about Jeremy. He's been so upset ever since we separated,' he says with a sigh.

Karen nods. 'Jeremy's whole world is upside down now, and he feels lost. You have disappeared from his life, and his older brother has left home too,' Karen replies.

'I know he needs me and I want to spend more time with him, but I have a very demanding job. I can't leave the office early. Often he is fast asleep when I come to see him after work, and his mother won't wake him. This arrangement isn't working, and it has to change.'

'You could talk to her about allowing him stay up a little later once or twice a week, and try your best to be there earlier,' Karen suggests.

'We both need to try harder to help him.'

I watch him staring out of the window as he fights to control his tears.

'It's so sad that at his young age, Jeremy has been caught up in our problems, and I worry he may be affected later.' He looks down, embarrassed, as he wipes away tears.

'Jeremy needs to feel important to you, and to spend time alone with you, whether it is talking, playing, or going out together. It isn't the length of time, but the quality of love and attention you give him,' Karen says.

They continue to talk, and Jeremy's father begins to look more relaxed.

'With my long hours of work, I haven't been an important part of his life, and I should've been. I'll make certain it changes. I know I will enjoy taking him to all the places that I missed out on at his age, and movies too.'

Karen smiles and offers help if he needs it.

I feel sorry for this tall, strong man who is as soft and unsure inside as little Jeremy. Maybe Jeremy and his father will grow closer and help each other. Humans seem far more complicated than I thought.

The room is empty at last. Karen sighs with tiredness, and runs her hands through her hair.

'Come to me, Beautiful,' she says.

I'm on her lap bathed in her aroma, and her gentle fingers know all the best tickle spots.

I am making my last nightly patrol of my territory. When I pass Samantha's chair, her shadow is waiting.

I thought she had crossed over the rainbow. Why is she here?

I sit patiently and watch. Her shadow moves gracefully, lowering itself onto the cushion. Slowly it rolls onto its back exposing its belly to me in trust. Then it lies motionless and eventually disappears. Cautiously, I approach the chair. I smell her faint scent. I understand. Samantha's shadow is assuring me that the house and Karen are mine completely now, and that she is finally leaving.

What a delightful *Cat Afternoon!* The sun is kissing the trees and flowers. I am warm and happy.

'Bella...Bella, my treasure,' Karen calls.

I pretend not to hear her. I am in a warm spot under the half-tree, and so comfortable.

'Where are you, Bella? Mia will be here soon!'

For Mia, I will leave my warm spot and go inside.

I sit in my basket in the therapy room and look through the window. Mia and her mother walk towards the door. Her mother walks slowly, carrying a strangely shaped case. Mia runs ahead of her. As Karen opens the door, Mia rushes inside.

'Karen, I have so much to tell you...and you too, Bella.'

She smiles, as she sits on the carpet next to me.

'I can't wait,' Karen says.

'Well, I went back to school. When the bullies started being nasty to me again, something wonderful happened. I imagined I was Bella with her beautiful ginger coat and her whiskers, and I turned my back on them. I didn't listen to a word they said, and it worked. They were fed up and left me alone.'

Karen laughs. Mia laughs, and her mum laughs too.

Laughter fills the room with joy. If only I could laugh too. Welcome to Catland, Mia!

'How wonderful, Mia. I'm so proud of you and Bella must be proud too,' Karen says.

'I'm so happy for Mia,' her mother says, as she gives Mia a hug.

Mia smiles, 'And there's more. Mrs Sands asked me to help two other girls who are being bullied. I'm teaching them to be like cats and ignore the bullies. I think it will work for them too.'

'Mia, you're amazing! You've turned your nervousness around,' Karen says. 'We need to celebrate with you playing your violin. I'm looking forward to hearing you play, and I bet Bella is too.'

Mia opens the strange looking case. Carefully she extracts a weird looking object with a long handle and a stick. She rests part of it on her shoulder and neck, and runs the stick across it.

Mee Meeeee Meee it whines. What a horrendous noise. It is like a sick cat meowing. I will try to stay in the room if I can, but I doubt my ears can put up with it. Just dreadful! I cannot understand why she plays the thing, but Karen is enjoying it. She has the same pleased look on her face when she is eating ice cream.

Finally, the Cat Torture is over. Karen and her Mum are clapping. Humans are indeed strange.

'My goodness, you are talented Mia...and at such a young age too,' I hear Karen say.

I need a rest after that noise.

They stand at the door talking for so long that I am almost asleep by the time Mia says goodbye to me.

It is early morning, and I watch the huge black dog from the house next door running along my fence and barking. He is incredibly stupid and barks during the day and at night. His owners should lock him inside. He has put me in a bad mood.

So, he hates cats does he? I will give him a good reason!

I wait until Karen opens the gate to my garden, then I chase him along the fence, but he does not stop barking. He is so angry that he sticks his long nose through the wire of the fence and growls a loud dog growl.

Ah hah! I zap his nose with my sharp claws. He runs away howling.

Stupid, stupid dog!

Inside, Karen is talking to a friend on the phone, telling her what I did to the dog next door.

I'm bored with the conversation, but my ears prick up when she talks about how smart cats are. I've known all along that we are smarter than dogs in many ways. And, she says we're almost as smart as very young Humans too. Well, that's interesting! She says that unlike dogs we don't persevere with tasks that we find boring or too frustrating. Of course not. We don't waste our time.

I look for a cool spot to stretch. The wonderful air machine blows cool through my fur. What a delight! I let every part of me cool down.

Suddenly, rain drums on the roof like huge rats dancing. Once, and only once, I went out into the rain. I rushed inside quickly with my fur coat dripping and stuck together.

It was one of my foolish mistakes. Rain is water after all, and anything to do with water except drinking it, has to be avoided.

I look for Karen, and find her on a cushion on the carpet. Her eyes are half-closed, like mine when I am happy. She is taking slow deep breaths. She is not asleep, but perhaps she is doing that relaxation thing she tells people about in the therapy room. I watch her carefully, as she stays in that position without moving. Now her eyes open slowly in a catlike way.

I am more and more certain that she was a cat in one of her past lives. Our understanding of each other is increasing every day.

She looks at me with a perplexed expression.

'Bella, it's strange, how sometimes you seem to grasp everything I'm saying...and doing.'

She's on the same Cat Mind-Line. Astonishing!

Someone is knocking on the door and breaking our intimate closeness.

It is our neighbour talking crossly. 'That cat of yours is vicious and should be done away with. She almost tore my dog's nose apart. I had to take him to the vet for stitches. Keep her under control or I will complain to the Council.'

'But, Bella is safely behind a fence and can't get out. What was your dog doing sticking his nose through the fence wire? He barks such a lot that I will complain about the noise. We cannot rest over the weekend. He should definitely be locked inside.'

The woman bangs the door in anger and walks off. Karen laughs so much that she looks as if she is crying.

Karen can be as naughty as a cat.

Jeremy and his mother are back to talk to Karen. He runs to my basket.

His words rush out. 'Hello, lovely Bella...my brother Laurie didn't come to visit me again like he promised and I miss him so much.' His eyes fill with tears.

'Jeremy, I'm sorry you didn't see Laurie, but I have some good news for you,' Karen says. 'Your dad came to talk to me this week. He loves you so much that he wants to make certain you are happy. He says that the two of you should spend more time together when you visit on weekends – to chat, have fun, eat out, watch sport, or go to a movie.'

Jeremy smiles for the first time.

'We'll see what happens this weekend,' his mother says.

Karen gives Jeremy's hand a reassuring squeeze. 'I'm sure you'll both have a great time together. I want to hear all about it next time I see you.'

After a long talk, Jeremy's mother stands ready to leave. 'Time to go, Jeremy.'

'Bye, Bella,' he says, with a wave to me.

Karen's phone rings. She answers sounding worried.

'Oh no! I'm so sorry to learn that Mia isn't well. She's in hospital? A burst appendix? And it happened suddenly? She was so happy and looked fine when she was here.' Karen is quiet while she listens. 'I'll call you soon to find out about her progress. I hope she feels much better soon. Send her love from me, and from Bella.'

Karen goes into the kitchen to boil water for tea.

It is strange how whenever Karen is worried, cross or

upset she makes tea before doing anything else.

Karen is working, but I am not needed in the therapy room. I go into my garden to find the brown cat waiting for me outside my fence. I'm pleased to see her. We would like to play, but we bump heads through the fence wire and chat instead. It is our best option, as Karen forgets to open the fence gate.

The sun is about to leave when I hear Karen calling, 'Dinner, Treasure.'

The atmosphere between Karen and Tony is tense again tonight. I hide behind the heavy, velvet curtain to feel safe, in case they argue. Karen goes to bed first. He drinks more dark liquid, and then follows her. I wait until the bedroom is quiet and then jump onto Karen's side of the bed. She is almost asleep, but Tony tosses restlessly.

'Can't you sleep darling?' Karen says.

He mutters a reply.

'Something worrying you?' She asks, as she turns on the light next to her bed.

'Work is tough at the moment. I'm still not sure whether I'll have a job in a few months,' he says.

No wonder Tony is stressed and unable to sleep. He talks to Karen about his problems at work. Though I can't understand any of it, I can tell by the tone of his voice that his difficulties are serious. Even though he dislikes me, I wish things were better for him.

She puts her arm around him, and he sighs.

'I love you my, darling,' she says.

He kisses her and says, 'I love you too.'

'You have incredible skills and experience on your side, I wish you wouldn't worry so much,' she reassures him.

Happy Cats! They kiss again and cuddle. He stretches to turn off the light.

'Time for you to go, Bella,' she says, giving me a gentle push.

I am in my garden waiting for the duck, but it does not visit me today. I call for my cat friends but they don't reply.

I am lonely and bored. I wish Karen would play with me. She is busy with her clients, but doesn't need me. When she is not working, she is on phone talking, or typing on the computer. I bite the tops of dried flowers and place them in a heap. It is something to do. Then I climb up and down the wire fence until I am tired. After scratching the base of the half-tree to leave my mark, I go inside to sleep on the big bed.

I am sitting near Karen, when she calls Mia's mother.

'How is Mia? Oh dear! So, she's not well yet, and has to stay in hospital for at least another week.' Karen sighs. 'I can imagine...it must be difficult for her. I will visit her later today.'

It is raining in my garden. Karen is visiting Mia, and I am alone in the house. I go to the big bed, but I don't feel like sleeping. Restlessly, I wander around the bedroom, sniffing corners, putting my head in the cupboards, and looking inside Karen's drawers that have her smell. I avoid anything belonging to Tony.

Karen's socks have her scent. I pull one pair out of the drawer, roll it on the carpet, and then carry it in my mouth to my chair in the sitting room. What fun! I go back to the cupboard to collect more socks, and place them all on my chair. I am tired now and fall asleep on the socks that smell of Karen.

At last, she is home. She does not notice me, but rushes to the kitchen to boil water for tea.

She is still ignoring me! I like to be acknowledged – at least given a pat the head to show she is pleased to see me.

I guess, Mia must be very sick and Karen is worried. I forget my irritation with her and forgive her, when I sense her sadness. I jump onto her lap, and rub the side of her face. Then, I wrap my tail around her arm to show her how much I love her.

'You can tell that I am sad, Bella. Poor little Mia is very sick, but the doctors are looking after her well.' She strokes my head tenderly.

I fall asleep on the couch, and wake later to hear her laughing.

'Sock thief!' She says, and laughs loudly. 'You are such a strange cat. You have lifted my worried mood.'

After two days of rain, the sun is shining again. In my garden, I hear a familiar *quark, quark.* What a thrill! My friend the duck is back, it ignores me and heads for a wide, empty, flower planter filled with rainwater. It dips and dives into the water. Then it shakes itself dry with a tail quiver. Droplets of water fall on me and I shudder.

At last, it remembers me, and our fun begins. It chases me around the garden on its strange, short legs and flaps its wings. I climb up the half-tree. It flies closer this time, pecking my nose and then my tail. It is mischievous today. I chase it until it flies up onto the fence wire. We rest, stare at each other, and then start the game again. I could play for longer, but it is up above me flying away.

Karen works all day with only a short break for lunch. It is late afternoon when I hear her door finally open. As she walks towards the kitchen, her footsteps are weary and heavy. She makes tea, and takes her cup to the couch. After a few sips she lies back. Her eyes close. I am next to her, but she is even too tired to stroke me. I nestle in her arms, purring loudly to give her some of my energy.

One thing about Karen that is not cat-like, and it worries me, is that she works too hard. If the Humans she is helping, their friends or family phone her for an appointment, she always agrees to fit them into her schedule. I wish she would learn to look after herself more. Some days her lunch break is too short and she eats too little. She isn't exercisng much on her bicycle either. If she did more exercise maybe she would have more energy. I love her lots, and want to her to be full of vitality like she used to be when I arrived.

I return to my favourite spot on Karen's side of the bed. I feel secure, warm and loved here. It is here on Karen's bed that I dream of my distant *Cat Past*.

I am with other cats in a huge, tall, stone building with many steps. The roof is higher than any house in our street. The Humans wear long clothes that touch the ground and walk slowly. They speak to us cats quietly with respect. There is a fire and the smell of burning meat in one part of the building. We wait and are fed scraps of the meat. Many of the Humans are gathered around the fire and call out in singing voices. Cats live in this place, and we are allowed to come and go as we please, as we are regarded as important and with a unique purpose.

This morning, Karen is up with the singing birds. In the kitchen, she has a cup of tea. Then she starts to cut up a large amount of meat and vegetables. There's a treat of meat for me too. She cooks all the food in two big pots. The smell is divine.

As Tony dresses for work, she fills small containers with the cooked food, and then puts them all into the very cold fridge.

Such early rising is unusual for Karen. She likes to sleep as late as possible. I can't remember her cooking in the early morning. Something must be about to happen.

While they eat breakfast, I sit under the table and listen.

'I've cooked enough food for you, darling. It's all labelled and in the freezer, and there is enough bread and fresh fruit to last.'

'You didn't need to do that, but thank you, my love,' he says.

Stinking, Rotting Rats! She's going away and leaving me... and I'll be alone with him.

'Bella eats tinned food and her small dry biscuits. All her food is on the side table. Just give her biscuits in the morning and open a tin for her dinner... and clean water daily, of course.'

He shrugs. 'It's okay, don't worry about me or Bella. We'll both be fine.'

'My friend Jodi has a key to the house. She'll pop in every day to change Bella's litter and spend some time with her.'

I will miss Karen, but I like Jodi. Just as well she's coming to visit me. At least she won't let me starve or have a dirty litter box.

'I wish I didn't have to go, but it's an important seminar about children's problems... and another two days at the sea will help me. Work has been busy this year and I'm so tired.'

'I want you to take a break. You need it. I haven't seen you as tired before. I'd come with you if I could, but I can't leave work at the moment. Don't worry about us, we'll be fine.'

Karen spends the rest of the morning tidying the house and working on the computer. After lunch we cuddle on the couch. She gives me extra loving strokes and kisses the top of my head.

'I love you, my precious,' she says. 'I won't be away for long.'

I breathe in her smell to try to hold it while she's gone.

Later, she puts papers and her flat computer in a case, and packs her clothes into a bigger one. By the evening, both cases sit near the front door.

The quarter moon is in the dark sky when the loud buzzer wakes us. Karen and Tony hurry to wash and dress. They drink hot liquid in the kitchen with toast, and Karen puts some of my biscuits in my bowl. She pats my head to say "goodbye". Tony carries the cases to the car and they are gone. I am alone in the house.

Suddenly I am scared. Once more, I'm that tiny kitten thrown near the garbage. What if she doesn't come back to me? I struggle to recall her smell. I notice that the door of her cupboard is open and I jump into the top drawer. Her smell is here, and I snuggle into the soft things she wears, and sleep. I wake when the sun leaves and lie on her side of the bed. I feel as if I have lost a huge chunk of my Catness.

Tony is home. The lights in my house are on and there is noise in the kitchen. Slowly, I leave the safety of the bedroom. I hide and watch Tony eat the food Karen cooked for him. Though he doesn't forget to open a tin of food for me, I am not hungry enough to eat it.

After talking on his hand phone and working on his

computer, he goes to the television room. Tonight he drinks extra bottles of dark liquid.

'Bella!' He calls, but I don't go to him.

'Bella, Bella, where are you?' He calls again and again.

'So, you're playing games.'

I come out of my hiding place and walk towards him.

I need to show him that I couldn't be bothered to play games with him. I'm surprised when he pats the couch for me to sit next to him. Then he pats his lap. Sit on Tony's lap... never! Cat Pride wouldn't allow it. But, I will sit on the other side of the couch. After all, he is the one who feeds me now.

The television room feels empty without Karen. Tony looks sad and finishes all the bottles of liquid. Perhaps he is lonely.

He's an only child, and both his parents died in a fire when he was a teenager. He has no one close except Karen and his grandfather, Pops. He watches sport, then falls asleep on the couch. Much later, he goes to bed.

I wake when Tony is in the shower. Then, in the kitchen, I hear him muttering about the food I didn't eat the night before. He leaves my old food in the dish, and empties some of my biscuits into my other bowl. No clean water.

After he leaves, I hear the back door open. It's Jodi. I run to her.

I say, *meow meow,* and jump up to greet her. She sits on the couch with me and we cuddle. She talks to me and even sings to me, and we cuddle again. I enjoy our closeness and her high pitched, cat-like voice when she sings. Her singing is so relaxing, that it almost puts me to sleep.

What a kind Human she is!

Jodi changes the litter in my box and cleans my food bowl. She gives me fresh water and opens a new tin of wet food for me. After a loving pat, she leaves.

At the door, she says, 'I'll be back again tomorrow, Bella.'

I eat and then sleep again. When I wake, I feel refreshed. I check my territory systematically and leave my scent on all the furniture and carpets. What a huge job! I make a point of leaving extra marks on all the scratch poles around the house. Washing myself is next, and I do a thorough job as mama taught me.

Jodi remembered to open the door to my garden, and I run out to check it as well. Nothing has changed apart from a few leaves on the ground that have fallen and a dead flower. I mark the rocks, plants and the half-tree with my scent. All is in order. My energy has returned. I run around the garden completing two circuits – less than usual, but good enough. After relaxing in the sun, I feel hungry and go indoors to eat again.

Cat Reflection! I relax on the big bed for a period of contemplation. This period without my Karen has taught me a lot. My Catness has returned, and I will not lose my Cat Survival and Cat Self-Preservation again. I cannot risk ever losing it again. Without it, the Essential Cat in me is gone. True Catness places a cat's need for food and the protection of territory before attachment to an owner.

But, Karen is an exceptional Human, and very Cat-like. I love her and place her high on my list for survival. No matter how powerful Catness is inside me, my love for Karen is intense and overwhelming. The thought of life without her is too frightening to even consider.

Each day without her follows the same pattern. Though I miss her a lot, I realise how fortunate I am to have Jodi visiting while Karen is away.

Tony might as well not be there.

Late one morning, the front door opens and Karen is back. Her voice is happy, her footsteps are light and energetic. She lifts me into her arms and hugs me. As much as I usually dislike being hugged, this one time I enjoy being so close to her.

Then she strokes me lovingly and talks to me in her sweetest voice. 'Bella, my treasure, my precious one, I'm so pleased to be home and with you again.'

After she has unpacked her clothes, she goes into the kitchen. She is pleased to find some of the food she cooked for Tony still in the very cold fridge.

'Great, it will be our dinner tonight, but I have something special for you,' she says, as she opens a tin of human tuna. Cat tuna doesn't taste nearly as good.

After dinner, we are all in the television room. Karen and Tony sit close to each other on the couch. Soon they are kissing, and forget I am there.

The ringing phone wakes me from a beautiful dream. What a pity to leave it. Perhaps I will visit it again.

Karen smiles as she talks. 'What good news! I'm so glad that Mia is home.' She listens, and then says, 'So, she wants to see Bella?'

I hear my name and wait.

'Of course, I will bring Bella to see her,' she says, glancing at the clock. 'I have some free time today. We will be there later.'

Karen boils water and drinks tea.

Another visit, wearing that dreadful harness and being

held captive in the plastic carry box, but anything for Mia.

It is only a short drive to Mia's house. Footsteps and then Mia's mother's voice.

'Thank you so much for coming and bringing Bella. I know that cats don't like leaving their homes, but I'm sure that Bella will help Mia to feel more cheerful. Mia is still weak and hardly eating.'

Karen follows Mia's mother, carrying me into a room. She opens the carry box to let me out. I check the room quickly. The bed has the sweet smell of Mia, but the rest of the room smells of a cat. I rub against the legs of a chair, roll on the carpet to make it safe, and rub the furniture. So far, all is under *Cat Control.* I am ready, sit quietly and wait.

Mia walks into the room slowly with her head down. She looks more fragile than the child who came to my house only a few weeks ago. Then, she had overcome the bullying and was full of life's force.

I notice her weakness and low energy. Once she is in her bed, she adjusts her pillows.

'Hello, Bella, you wonderful, darling cat! Thank you so much for coming to visit me...and you too, Karen, for bringing her.'

I jump onto Mia's bed and move towards her. She pats my head, and tickles the tender spot under my chin.

She whispers to me, 'You understand Bella. I knew you understood from the first time I saw you. You know everything.'

I have a warm connecting feeling inside. This child knows more about cats than most Humans I have come across. She is extremely cat-like.

I snuggle closer and purr. She smiles. Karen is sitting in the room watching. Touched by the love between us, her eyes mist with tears. Then, she tip toes out of the room and leaves us. In the background I hear Karen and Mia's mother talking about us. Then everything drifts away as we fall asleep together.

We wake when Mia's mother comes into the room carrying food and water. She has some delicious, pink fishy things in a bowl for me.

'Prawn meat especially for Bella,' Karen says. 'She'll adore that.'

Prawns! Is that what these wonderful bits of fish are called. Yumow!

After Mia eats she smiles. 'Being with Bella is wonderful. She's such a special cat,' she says.

'I wish you could have a cat of your own, Mia, but you know that your dad is allergic to cats. Remember how sick he was when we had Chi?'

Mia looks away, trying not to cry.

'As it is, I'm taking a risk bringing Bella into the house. She's short haired and that makes a big difference. She is only in your room, so I doubt your dad will be affected.'

'What about a dog with woolly hair, like a poodle or a hairless cat? They don't cause allergy problems.' Karen suggests.

Mia looks past her mother at me, and shakes her head. 'I don't want a dog or cat without fur.'

Mia's mother and Karen move away from the bed to talk.

Then Karen says, 'When you feel better, you can visit Bella and play with her.'

'I can drop you off after school to be with Bella. What do you think of that?' Her mother adds.

'That will be wonderful,' Mia says.

'It's a great idea. Bella could do with more company. I'm busy a lot of the time and she is lonely,' Karen replies.

Mia claps her hands with joy. 'Oh Mum and Karen, thank you!'

I watch Mia smile, and I feel happy too. I love Mia and will enjoy visits from her.

I am asleep in a sunspot behind the curtains, when I hear Karen's footsteps.

'I know you're there behind the curtain, Bella. I can see your tail,' she says. 'We will be visiting Helena soon. She is at home recovering, and longs to see you. Sorry, my sweetie, but you'll have to wear your harness again.'

Stinking Rats! I wore the harness yesterday to visit Mia and my tummy feels tender. I refuse to wear that contraption again. I flick my tail several times in strong disapproval.

Karen is too close for me to escape. My claws grip the carpet, but she grabs me firmly. Though I struggle, she ignores my reluctance, puts the harness on, and pushes me inside the carry box. A lock snaps closed. I am a prisoner.

Karen is as dominant and manipulative as a cat. She can be devious too. More proof of her Catness.

Meeeeow. Meeeeow! Meeeeeeeow let me out!

'Shush, shush, Bella. We are doing this for Helena. You like her a lot.'

She's right, I do like Helena, but I dislike this plastic carry box. It has a strange smell and the windows are little holes, but I will put up with the inconvenience for Helena.

I know I'm complaining, but we are in the car now, stopping and starting, and my harness feels too tight around my middle. I hate traveling, especially when I'm locked up. The movement and smell of the carry box makes me dizzy.

At last we stop completely. As before, Lily is waiting for us.

'Mum's breathing has improved a little, and she has been out of bed for short periods. She hasn't stopped talking about Bella and how much she loves her.'

Well, at least my misery has a purpose!

This time Helena is sitting in a soft chair. She smiles and claps her hands.

'Oh, Karen, you've brought Bella!'

Karen removes my lead and I jump onto Helena's lap.

'Take Bella's harness off. She doesn't need it in here,' Helena says.

Phew! Thank you Helena.

Helena has some tiny biscuits for me. I gobble them up. Then she strokes me from the very top of my head and down my nose, with her old hands that know and love cats. As I purr happily, her head slips back against the chair, and she sleeps. I sleep too.

When we wake, Helena's breathing is easier.

I wonder how I help her, but somehow I do. That is what's important.

Lily has the scrumptious fish food waiting for me again. It seems even tastier this time. I lick my lips and look around for more, but there is none.

'Helena has decided that she wants a cat. She adores Bella, but Bella can't visit every day,' Lily says. 'An older cat will suit us. We aren't able to care for a kitten.'

Karen smiles. 'What an excellent idea! I am sure a cat will be a good companion and make a big difference.'

The drive home is in heavy traffic. It is almost night when we arrive home. The house is in darkness.

'Tony is late again tonight,' Karen says with a sigh. Instead of the hot tea she usually drinks, she pours herself half a glass of a strong, dark smelling liquid from a tall bottle in the cabinet. She drinks it quickly. Then she lies on the couch and sleeps.

Tony's footsteps wake us. 'Hello...where are you?'

Karen sits up and rubs her eyes. 'Sorry, but I haven't made dinner, or even given Bella her food.'

'Feed the cat and change. We're going out. It's time we had a date,' he says.

The time spent with Helena has devoured most of my energy. I am too tired to do more than nibble at my food.

When they return, they are laughing and kissing. With a warm feeling, I fall back to sleep.

I am asleep on the big bed. It doesn't take long for me to dream. The bed is my perfect dream place.

I am travelling backwards in time, to another life.

In the rosy dawn, farm animals wake. I am in a barn with other cats and three pregnant cows, soon to give birth. The cows are enormous and make big poos. With their large feet and poos, it is best to keep away from them.

The Humans, who own the farm, live in a nearby stone house. The woman likes cats. Every morning she places a big bowl of milk and bread for us cats on the steps of the house. There's a struggle to be first for food. Only the strongest cats find a place at the food bowl. I eat from the bowl every day. As I am a good mouse catcher, the woman likes me and calls me Fast One. Sometimes she throws me a bit of meat as a treat.

After eating I sleep all day.

Darkness surrounds me now. Tonight as on other nights, I hunt for mice in the barn. Mice have their nests here. They eat the farmer's store of grain and feed their young.

A young mouse I have just caught dangles from my jaw and I eat most of it quickly. I enjoy hunting, watching, stalking and pouncing on these little creatures. The young ones make a succulent, tasty meal. I leave the rats for the others. They are larger creatures, tougher to digest and not at all tasty.

Though it is cold tonight, we are not invited inside the human's house, to sit next to their fire like the dogs. For warmth, I lie beside my friend, a small, striped cat. We trust each other, and though we hunt alone, we often eat and sleep together. Here on the farm, there are many cats – enough of us to form a colony. Fights break out when one cat attempts to dominate the others.

Unlike the dogs who are dependent on the farmer, we come and go as we please. As pack animals, the dog's leader controls the other dogs in the pack, and decides where to find shelter. Puppies are at a disadvantage if the pack moves. At twelve weeks old, they are still learning about the world around them, and how to navigate it. A kitten of the same age is more mature. Their mamas teach them to hunt and they are able to live independently.

We cats live on farms for our security, food and warmth. The farmers need us to kill their mice and rats – a good arrangement. But, we are constantly on the look out for dogs. We run fast and climb, but if caught by a dog with their powerful jaws it's the end of us.

'Bella, there you are, asleep. Come, I need you in the therapy room.'

I wake slowly, taking my time to go to Karen.

I think of my dream. I'm fortunate to be living in now time, here in Karen's house, and not with many other cats in a barn surviving on mice. I have nibbled the occasional mouse, but I prefer human food, like chicken or fish.

The house is still apart from the sounds of Karen and Tony sleeping. Onto the big bed, I jump and lie nestled in Karen's arms.

When I wake, bright sunlight greets me. 'Happy birthday Bella,' it says, as it sends warming light to me. It knows that today is my special day, but my Humans are still asleep. I touch Karen's face with my paw, but she turns around, ignores me and goes back to sleep. I won't try to wake Tony, as his arm will swat me like one of those black flying things.

I am two years old today. Two years ago, Karen rescued me in the park. I cuddle up to her on the pillow, lie on her long hair…and wait. I grab a few stands of her hair, and suck them. Tired of waiting for them to wake, I nip her lightly on her arm. Her eyes open, at last.

She yawns. 'Bella, my precious…happy birthday!'

She stretches and is out of bed slowly. I run ahead of her, wanting her to hurry. In the kitchen, she opens the big cupboard.

'A present for your birthday, Treasure,' she says in the gentle, purring voice she uses only for me.

Out comes a coloured stick with a long, shimmering tail and a bell. One shake and it is magic. It dances and leaps across the floor, up to the table and along the wall. The tiny bell rings too. Such fun! I chase it until I can't chase any longer. Then I lie on the carpet to rest.

'A special birthday treat for you too, my Bella,' she says as she opens a tin. The smell is tantalising and the room sings with the divine smell. *Tuna, tuna tuna!* My delicious birthday food is gone in minutes. Of course I want more, but more does not come.

She strokes me tenderly. I jump up to her, rub my head against her, and then wrap my tail around her arm. She knows I am saying 'thank you'.

She tickles the top of my head and gently touches the tips of my ears. 'Come back to bed, Bella, my sweetie,' she says. 'It's Sunday and we can sleep longer today. Later some of our friends are coming. We're having a fun birthday party for you!'

A party for me? There will be strange Humans trying to touch me and pick me up, but there will be a lot of food and possibly gifts for me.

After more sleep, Karen rushes to the kitchen to make final preparations for the guests. Tony moves the big table into the sitting room. He sets out cups and saucers, while Karen fills platters with fruit, cake and biscuits. She makes fresh sandwiches and soon the table is laden. She places a bowl of flowers in the centre of the table.

'Now, it looks beautiful for your party, Bella,' she says with a happy smile.

'Come Bella, one last thing. I have a pretty, pink bow for the birthday girl.'

I battle with her, as she ties the bow to my collar, but I give in to please her.

Rats! I will tug at it and bite it off later, to be free of it.

When the visitors arrive, Karen carries me into the front room.

'Happy birthday, Bella, you wonderful, spoilt kitty,' one Human says.

I do not like the sound of her voice. I am about to turn my back on her, when she pulls out a little, bouncing ball on a string. 'A present for you, sweet, darling,' she says.

'Don't you look gorgeous Bella, birthday girl,' another says carrying a shiny toy with a long feather.

Others come with birthday gifts for me too. They all laugh a lot about me, a cat, having a birthday party.

I don't think it's funny! It's my birthday, after all. Why shouldn't I have a party?

Karen brings more food to the table – salty, fishy things and a huge cake too. The smell is bliss. She gives me some fish on a plate. The flavour tastes strange, and I leave it. There will be more food to come. While they talk, I smell enticing, milky sweetness. I spring onto the table to follow the aroma. I find the source on the cake. It is soft, thick and white. I lick it quickly. It's *Yumow!*

'Oh no! She's found the cream! Off the table, now, Bella!' Karen says in her cross voice.

One of the visitors says, 'Come on Karen, don't be mean to your kitty. Give her some cream. It's her birthday after all!'

Karen scoops a generous spoonful onto a plate for me.

'There you are Princess, Enjoy!'

Like all good things, it's gone too quickly.

Finally, they all leave.

My birthday is over. I wish it would go on for longer.

I find a gift of flowers and leaves from a friend of Karen's in the kitchen. I enjoy shredding the leaves with my claws.

'Naughty cat!' Karen shouts. 'Time for you to go into the garden.'

I go through my door very slowly.

Rat's Poo! She'll be sorry for talking to me in that tone... and on my birthday too.

I am still peeved with Karen.

When she calls me to the therapy room, I pretend I can't hear her. After she talks to me kindly, strokes me from head to tail several times, I forgive her for talking rudely to me and follow her.

'You can be so picky and sensitive,' she says.

A mother and her young child enter the room. The child is crying and clutches his mother's hand. I listen to the mother's voice. She is nervous and talks quickly.

'Dane is five and an only child. He is bright, but shy and afraid of being left alone. Most nights he wakes with nightmares, and runs crying to our bed. He's so tired and upset in the morning that he won't go to kinder.'

Karen listens to the mother and talks to the child in her gentle voice.

Rotting Rats! The poor child is scared. He is seeking love and security. When I lie next to Karen at night, it is warm and cuddly. I feel safe. His bad dreams must be scary. No wonder he runs to his parents' bed.

My Karen is incredible. So patient! I don't know how she listens for so long to each one of the distressed Humans who come to see her.

She takes the child's hand. 'Come and see the kitty, Dane. Her name is Bella. She is so pleased that you came to visit us today.'

The child approaches me with tentative steps.

'Hello, Bella,' he says in a small, scared voice.

'Sit next to Bella for a while. She likes children and won't hurt you, so don't be scared of her,' Karen says.

Dane sits on the carpet next to my basket. Tears fill his eyes and run down his face. I know what to do. Slowly, I move from my basket, sit next to him and gently put my paw on his leg. Hesitantly, he touches me. I purr and look up at him. Gradually he stops crying.

While Dane is with me, Karen asks his mother questions about him – when and where he was born, and if he's had any illnesses. The questions continue about Dane's behaviour at home, his family, and past experiences. She seems to ask all the Humans who come to see her so many questions.

Dane's mother looks down to hold back her tears. 'I think that Dane is upset about the fire next door three months ago.'

She talks fast, so I have to listen hard.

'Dane's friend Troy lived in the house next door to us. The two boys played together and were close friends. One night, there was a fire in Troy's house. Though his father managed to carry Troy and his sister out safely, his mother was badly burned. By the time the firemen put the blaze out, the house was destroyed. We were lucky, our house didn't catch alight'. She stopped for a moment to take a deep breath. 'It was a terrible night. We all watched Troy's mother taken to hospital in an ambulance. The hospital treated her for weeks, but finally she died. It was devastating for the family and Dane hasn't been the same child since the fire.'

'No wonder Dane is having nightmares. The fire must've been a terrifying experience, and for such a young child. Then the death of his friend's Mum, must've been so upsetting for him...and difficult to understand,' Karen says, looking concerned.

'Dane doesn't talk about it, but I see him sitting staring through the window at the open, black space where the house next door once stood.'

Karen talks to Dane softly. 'Are you and Bella making friends?'

He nods. 'She's a lovely kitty.'

'I can tell that she likes you too. She understands, so talk to her if you want to.'

Dane nods again and pats me gently.

I move closer and purr loudly.

'You're such a lovely kitty!' He says.

Dane's mother sighs, 'Unfortunately, Troy's dad bought a new house quite a distance away, so the boys don't see each other often now.'

'I know Dane hasn't wanted to go to kinder lately, but the routine, activity and being with other children will help him enormously,' Karen suggests. 'I hope he will go back soon.'

'I will try to encourage him to go,' his mother says.

They begin to discuss ways to help Dane to recover. One of them is establishing a daily routine at home, so that his life is more predictable and he can feel more secure.

While they talk about building his confidence, I fall asleep. By the time Karen wakes me, Dane and his mother have left. She tells me that there will be another child coming soon.

Grrrrrrrr! She is too busy today and I am busy too. I haven't even had Cat Time to check my house and garden, or wash myself properly.

Tony and Karen are arguing again. Tonight they have the worst of their arguments. Their loud voices yelling at each other scare me. I run to the other end of the house to hide, but I can still hear them.

A wild, shouting storm has hit my house. What in Catland is happening?

Later, when I creep out, Tony is sleeping in the second bedroom. Karen is alone in the big bed. I hear her crying and go to her. As I lie next to her, she stokes me. Gradually she stops crying.

'You know everything, my precious.' She kisses the top of my head and strokes the thick fur around my neck.

In the morning, Tony comes back to the big bedroom and they talk.

'I'm sorry I upset you, my darling. You know how much I love you,' he says.

'I love you too...we are both to blame,' she says.

He nods and gives her a kiss.

'We are both overtired, working too hard, and too much. I am missing my dad and sisters. I would like to see them, and stay with them for a while. It would be a great holiday,' she says.

'I can take the time off work in about two weeks. It will be perfect for a break,' he says, giving her another kiss. 'Let them know we're coming.'

Thank Cats Above! The storm is over.

This morning Karen is not working.

'A lady is coming to clean today,' she says, as she grabs her handbag and rushes out of the house. 'Goodbye, Sweetie! Please be good!'

She is in such a hurry to leave the house that she forgets to give me food. This is the second time it has happened.

Withholding food is an extremely serious Cat Offense.

Something important must be happening for a lady to come and clean.

Footsteps. The front door opens. A woman I have not seen before enters the house. I hide in a corner, observing her as she collects long sticks, brushes and bottles from the tall cupboard .

She notices me. 'Out of the way, Puss,' she says gruffly.

I   watch as she sweeps and cleans all the surfaces with the stuff from the bottles, and uses a long stick with feathers, that must've belonged to a big, black bird. Then, she uses the noisy vacuum on the carpet to remove my hair. Later, she shakes the cushions to make them full.

Please, don't touch my favourite cushion. No luck, she shakes it too.

Save Cat's Ears! She sings out of tune while she works, and ignores me. The noise of her singing is awful.

I don't want to be noticed, as I have my own plans concerning the food cupboard. She leaves the door of the food cupboard in the kitchen slightly ajar. Karen always closes it. I am hungry, push the door open, and jump onto the lowest shelf. There isn't anything interesting here. The middle shelf has little hard tins that smell of fish. I struggle to open one with my claws, but I am wasting my time. A box of my favourite biscuits – the ones Karen gives me for a treat is open. I push it until the box falls on its side. I eat quickly, delighting in a mouthful of biscuits, until the woman notices me in the cupboard.

'Get out of there!' She lifts the broom in an attempt to hit me with it. I arch my back, bristle and snarl at her, ready to attack.

'You nasty cat,' she yells, drops the broom and moves back.

Her lucky day! I'd have bitten and scratched her if she'd dared to hit me.

She won't worry me again now, but she's tidied away the tasty biscuits. At last, the door bangs. She has gone.

Karen is back. She sniffs the air and checks that the house is clean.

I ignore her, and do not go to her when she calls, so that she knows and learns. She has left me without food all morning. Finally she notices my bowl is empty.

'I'm so sorry my treasure,' she says, as she pours pebbles into my bowl.

I love her, and forgive her, but this is happening far too often lately.

All is quiet again in *Catland*, but I sense that something is about to happen. Karen is walking fast, carrying sheets and pillows to the back room. Now, she is making the bed.

I keep watch through the window in the front room. A car arrives. Karen's mother, Liz walks slowly to the front door using her stick. Before she knocks on the door, she notices piles of leaves at the front of the house and shakes her head disapprovingly. Then, with her stick she clears away the leaves from the door. Once Liz is inside, she greets Karen and they hug and kiss. Karen collects her mother's suitcase and a bag from the car.

Oh no! She's going to stay for a few days. Liz is not my favourite Human.

Liz opens the bag, and out comes a present. Karen tears off the paper with a happy shout. Again she kisses her mother.

Great Rats! Get on with it!

I wait quietly for Liz to spot me in the corner of the room.

'That cat of yours is here! You know I don't like cats. They give me allergies. Can't you lock her up somewhere?'

'No Mum, I can't...and I won't. Bella is part of the family. Avoid her. She knows you don't like her. Anyway, she has short hair and you won't have any allergy problems.'

I love you so much Karen. Liz will have to learn that this is my territory. But, I will try as hard as I can to get rid of her fast.

Karen spends longer than usual in the kitchen cooking a special meal for her mother. While cooking, she gives me pieces of soft, juicy meat. Of course I want more.

Then she says to me in her stern voice, 'Bella, Mum doesn't like cats. Please stay away from her tonight, or I'll have to lock you out. You know that you won't like it.'

Rat's Poo! My ears are back, my tail swaying wildly. My whiskers even twitch in annoyance. This is my house too!

Tony arrives late and Karen makes apologises to her mother for him. I sense that Tony doesn't like Liz either. He hardly talks to her and he drinks more dark liquid from his bottles than usual. Now he's asleep on the couch.

'Sorry about Tony,' Karen says to her mother. 'He works hard and his job is stressful. He is tired most nights.'

Karen, you're telling fibs! He is sleeping on purpose, like I do when I am bored with one of the Humans who visit you.

At last they all go to bed.

Happy Cats! This is my chance to get rid of Liz. I creep up to see what she is doing. If I can slip into her room she will detest it, and me. Hopefully she will leave early. But, bang – the door closes.

The next morning, they all dress early, and eat breakfast hurriedly. They must be going out. Oh no, Liz has closed the door of the room again!

This time, Karen checks that I have enough food and water, and they leave. Lovely! I have the whole house to myself, to place my mark all over the clean house, and to sharpen my claws. I can sleep as long as I desire on the big, soft bed.

After eating I go outside. I have fun chasing a mouse around the garden, but it escapes. Then I try to chase a rat, a far bigger prize, but not to eat. I'm unlucky again. It has disappeared under the house.

I sit in a sun patch wondering what to do next, when I hear a whirring sound. The duck is back to play. It hovers over me, teasing me. I turn about to use my claws to catch it, but I stop myself. I don't want to hurt it. We play until the sun slides behind the clouds.

Then, I hear the car. They are home. I greet Karen quickly and hide again.

Great Happy Cats! Liz has forgotten about me. She leaves the door of her room open while she changes. I slip inside the room and stare at her. Then, knowing she will hate it, I brush against her leg.

She screams, 'Karen, Karen get this cat of yours away from me!'

Meeeow wow! That was the best fun I've had all day!

'Bella...you're a naughty, naughty cat,' Karen says in her cross voice. 'I know exactly what you're up to. You're trying to freak Mum out.'

Cat Punishment. A day of being locked up in the tiny room with the soap powder and dirty washing. I'm in prison with just my food, water and litterbox.

In the afternoon, Karen opens the door to my garden to let me play, but makes sure I can't come into the house.

Meanwhile, I'm making plans.

Tonight in the laundry again, I smell wafts of their dinner and hear them talking. I can tell a lot from my laundry prison. It's Liz's birthday, and they are singing. How absolutely dreadful it sounds. To celebrate, Karen has bought a cake. Their glasses clink and their voices become louder.

When Karen comes to feed me, she strokes me all over and calls me her precious. She smells strange from all the food and drink, but I ignore that. I am focussed on the laundry door. After stroking me she forgets to close it.

Now's my chance! I slip out, hide and wait. While they are eating cake and drinking, I slink along the floor so they won't notice me. The door to Liz's room is slightly open. What a thrill! I push the door open. Now, I search for the perfect spot. I leave a dark, smelly present for her on the carpet next to her bed. Then, I return to my laundry prison to sleep.

I have accomplished my aim.

A loud scream wakes me. It's Liz screaming.

'That evil cat of yours has made a huge, stinking poo on my carpet! I think I'm going to faint.'

'Sit down Mum, and don't get upset. I'll clean it up,' Karen says calmly. 'I'll make you some tea.'

'She's a nasty cat. You should get rid of her.'

While Karen cleans away my poo and sprays disinfectant on the carpet, she talks to her mother in the soft voice she uses for me.

'Mum, Bella knows you don't like her. She doesn't like you either. While you've been here she was locked in the laundry, and hated it. This is her way of paying you back.'

'I don't care, it's utterly revolting...disgusting! I'm going home tomorrow!'

Happy, Happy Cats! It worked. Wonderful!

I eat, and then hide again. Karen will be very cross.

The next morning, there's a lot of noise. From my prison, I hear Liz packing her suitcase. Karen is helping her. They eat and drink together, and talk. Then, Karen carries the suitcase through the front door.

Ecstatic Cats! Liz has gone.

Karen lets me out of prison. I forget my time spent locked up, run to her and roll over on my back for tickles.

'You're a naughty, naughty cat, but I love you so much,' she says. 'I'm glad she's gone too. I'm so busy, and I couldn't do a thing with her here.'

'Where are you, Bella? Time for work,' she calls, and I follow her.

Dane and his mother are back to talk to Karen.

When Dane sees me, he runs towards me. 'Hello Bella', he says, stroking my coat. He takes my paw and kisses it.

Happy to see him, I purr and touch his leg with my paw to tell him that I am returning his affection .

Dane's mother says that the routine they have been following has given him a little more security, but he is still having nightmares, and he won't talk about the fire. She looks worried, as she tells Karen that Dane still refuses to go back to kinder.

Karen turns towards Dane. 'While your Mum and I are chatting, Dane, talk to Bella. She understands everything.'

Karen tells children that I understand everything to encourage them to talk to me, and they seem to believe her. I don't mind if it helps them. Helping is my job.

I hoped that listening to Human's troubles in the therapy room would increase my understanding of them, but from my Cat View they still remain inexplicable. I sense their joy and sadness, and I feel concern for them. But, even when my whiskers turn grey, I doubt I will have deeper insight into their true Humanness.

Dane moves closer. As he strokes me, he tells me about the huge flames, the smell of burning and the screams during the fire. Suddenly, he stops talking and begins to cry again. I put my paws around his neck to give him a *Cat Hug*.

Poor Dane! Perhaps next time he will tell me the rest of his story.

Karen and Dane's mother are discussing family activities that might help him – picnics, visits to the beach and movies, when he interrupts them. 'Mum, please, please.... can I have a cat like Bella?'

Dane's mother looks uncertain.

'That's a good idea. A kitten or a puppy might help Dane,' Karen says. 'He would have a furry friend to talk to and play with, and to sleep with at night. There are lots of animals without homes at rescue centres.'

'You're right Karen, a pet would probably help him,' his mother says. 'I will talk to his dad about a pet tonight.'

Autumn/Fall

Days are shorter, and the sun's warmth is weaker. Grass in my garden is dry, the ground is hard, and all the flowers have shrivelled and gone. Leaves on the trees are changing into brilliant colours and beginning to fall in heaps.

I chase mice and other creatures that hide amongst the crunchy leaves. Kicking them into the air as I play is fun. Most birds are leaving for warmer places. At least they won't be here to taunt me.

Today the Duck visits me. While we play, it watches the sky. Suddenly we are in virtual darkness, and the sounds of many ducks surround us. Immediately my duck friend stops playing. It waddles towards me, says *quark, quark*, before it takes off to join the others. I watch it fly away until it disappears into the mass of black.

Cold air blows through my fur coat and I shiver. Swirls of wind arrive and shake the leaves off trees. I am safe undercover and watch the leaves fall, until a storm of dust arrives. I run inside through my special door with itchy eyes.

'Hurry and eat your breakfast, Treasure,' Karen says. 'We are visiting the hospital this morning to see Tamara, a young girl who is very sick. She loves cats, and her doctor wants you to spend some time with her.'

There is no point complaining about wearing the harness and lead. Karen says I look professional in it, but I know she is trying to pacify me. Like a cat, she can be so manipulative. At least I am wearing it today for a good reason.

Karen takes me through the hospital that smells of vile antiseptics. We stop at the place they call the Cancer Ward. I hear the voices of children through my carry box and smell sickness. Karen opens my box, and holds me in her arms. Everything around us is white. A sick child lies in a bed in front of us.

'Hi Tamara,' Karen says. 'Bella is here to visit you. She knows how much you love cats.'

A tiny smile starts to form on the thin child's pale face. Her hand stretches towards me.

'That's great! Please, Bella come to me.'

'I will fetch a blanket for the cat to lie on. Just a minute,' a nurse says.

Soon I am on Tamara's bed purring.

I sense that Tamara is extremely ill. I must try as hard as I can to help her.

I purr loudly and nestle in her arms. She holds me and closes her eyes.

'You remind me of my cat, Sherry, at home. They won't allow her to visit me. She is too old and sick, like me,' she says with teary eyes. 'I don't know if I will see her again.'

I lie with Tamara as she strokes me. She talks to me about all the things she enjoyed when she was well, and even laughs occasionally. I fall asleep next to her until the sound of loud talking wakes me. Humans dressed in white stand around asking Karen about me. Karen says that they are doctors.

'A little ginger angel,' one says.

Karen laughs 'Bella is an exceptionally loving cat with a healing gift, but definitely no angel.'

When Tamara wakes, she strokes me again before Karen puts me back in my carry box.

'Please bring Bella to visit me again,' she asks.

Cat Alert! I guard the television room, as I listen to sounds of movement in the ceilings and in the walls of my house. Rats! I am certain of it. I can hear their high-pitched squeaks and whines, and their gnawing of the woodwork. They are an invading army in *Catland*, constantly on the move.

As I prepare for war, I sharpen my claws on my scratch post until they are effective weapons. I prowl and check my territory.

The cooler weather has probably brought them into the warm house through cracks in the roof tiles.

What if they find a crack in the ceilings or walls and come into my house? I must not allow myself to even think of an army of filthy rats in my house. If they manage to find a way inside, they could leave their poo on the carpets, beds and in my basket. Though I dislike the taste of rat, I am a skilled hunter. Unfortunately, this time there are too many of them for me to destroy alone. What a situation for a cat to face!

Here I am worried about a rat invasion, and Karen and Tony are completely unaware of the danger we face. When Tony eventually notices a few strange noises and banging he blames it on changes in the weather. What can I do? I try hard to focus their attention on this problem with loud, meows and constant stares at the ceiling, but they take no notice.

As the rat population grows unhindered, the sounds of their high-pitched communication and scurrying increases. I feel helpless – a useless cat, fearing the loss of my territory.

'Bella is acting strangely, but I have no idea why,' Karen says to Tony.

Tony shrugs. 'She does crazy things sometimes.'
He must be deaf...and not very smart.
Today Karen is cooking a lot of food for a friend's party.

Thank All Cats! She is hunting for a large dish in a tall cupboard when at last she hears high-pitched squeaks above her.

'Tony, come and listen! I think there are rats in the ceiling – lots of them. No wonder Bella was acting so strangely.'

After hearing the rat sounds, he rushes to the shops to buy rat poison. He is back now, and throws the rat poison into the ceiling.

And about time too! Humans are so slow to react and have such poor hearing. At least, I won't have the responsibility of fighting this invading army alone..

Today, weak sunlight streams into a quieter, safer house. What a pleasure!

What is happening now in Catland?

Karen and Tony are selecting clothes from their cupboards and putting them on the bed. Then, Tony carries suitcases into the bedroom .

Stinky, Rotting Rats! A sick feeling hits my tummy. I know exactly what is happening. They are packing their clothes to go away. This must be the holiday Karen said they needed.

I remain hidden under the bed all morning and part of the afternoon. Then, I move to the corner of the room behind the curtain where they won't see me. I hear them calling me, but I ignore them. Karen eventually finds me, lifts me up, and they both force me into the carry box.

Much worse is to come.

They put me in the back of the car.

Meeooooow. Meeeooow!

After a bumpy ride in foul smelling traffic, Karen says, 'We're here, Bella. You're going to have a lovely holiday at the cattery!'

I have no idea what a cattery is – and just as well.

She carries me inside, but I see almost nothing through the tiny holes in my box. The sound and smell of too many cats in a small confined space is overwhelming. Once my carry box is open, I am in a small cage with a wire around it. The cage has a downstairs area for my food and a poo box, and an upstairs to sleep. Karen places my own basket in the cage, so that I will be comfortable and have something familiar with me. She delves into her handbag to produce a vest she has worn, and puts it into the basket. The vest carries her scent – a reminder that she will be with me. After stroking me several times, she whispers "goodbye".

She lingers and talks to me in her sweet voice.

Tony says gruffly, 'Come on Karen, leave the cat now, and hurry up!'

I watch them go and cry inside. What if they leave me here and never ever come back for me?

'Bella, this is your place now while your family are on holiday. I will look after you,' a Human cat worker says.

Cat Instinct! Grrrrrrrrrr! I dislike this Human immediately. I sense that she dislikes me...and all cats. Why in Catland is she working in a cattery? Can't she find another job? I will have to be extremely careful in all my interactions with her.

I lie far back in my basket on Karen's vest and try to relax, but I can't.

Meow, meow, meow I call over and over. Let me out, and take me home.

Food and water are in the cage, but I am not hungry. I stay in my basket all day and through the night. I slink out only to go to the litterbox.

Surely Karen wouldn't have put me in this place if she had known how miserable I would be. I keep telling myself that she loves and cares for me, and hope that she will come back to take me out of this awful place. But the days pass, and she doesn't come.

In the early light, I edge out of my basket. Many cats before me have left their mark on the cage. To feel safer in the cage, I know that I must cover their scent. I listen to the sounds of other cats around me calling, asking for food, or begging for a run. Their overpowering smell has me rushing back to my basket. When I venture out again, I rub my body on the cage wire to remove some of the foreign scent. I am unable to settle, and jump from the top of the cage to the bottom, again and again. The horrible cat worker comes to check up on me. She tries to touch me, and I hiss at her. Before I know it, instinctively my paw armoured with sharp claws is poised ready to scratch her. She curses loudly, quickly withdrawing her hand.

She won't dare to touch me again. At least now she knows how I feel about her. She is horrible, and so I will call her Horrible from now on.

Cats face me, and are on both sides of my cage. A black and white female Tabby is on one side and a handsome striped male on the other. Opposite is a pale, fluffy Persian.

'He's a Bengal,' I hear Horrible say, pointing to the handsome stripped cat.

Black and White is aggressive. She hisses, shows her claws, and then turns her back on me. Handsome Male rubs himself on the wire.

He wants to be friends. *Purr pree prup prup* welcome, he says. He has a much larger cage than mine, and part of a tree to climb. Not Fair! I watch him climb the tree. He is fast and athletic!

Persian opposite is long-haired with a magnificent, cream coat. She is a vain, show-off who is not interested in communicating with any of us. Horrible says she is a prize winner.

A young Human comes to talk to me. His voice is kind, and immediately I like him.

'Cool it, pussy cat,' he says. 'You'll be fine. You won't have to even see that woman you don't like. Many of the other cats dislike her too. I will look after you until your owners come to pick you up...and they won't forget you, I promise.'

I allow him to pat my head.

With this Human, I will be safer.

'You can come out for a walk if you want to.' He opens the cage door, but I stay in my basket.

'That's fine, you can come out tomorrow...as you like.'

He puts down some wet food for me, but I am not hungry. Handsome Male eyes my food. He is hungry.

The lights go out. The other cats call, and in the dark I feel scared. At last I sleep. Tonight, my dreams are not of the distant past. They are about my house, my garden and Karen. I wake when the pale sun shines onto my basket.

The young Human cleans my litterbox. I see Horrible walk past. She looks away, disliking me.

The young Human talks to me, as he opens the cage door. 'Come to me. Come, Pretty Girl!'

I put my head out. Slowly I move towards him. He allows me to smell his hand before he touches me. I can tell that he respects cats. He strokes my head, and then the rest of me. I start to feel calmer. I know he cares about me.

He puts my food bowl and water down in front of me.

'Eat Sweet Girl.'

I eat a few of the strange tasting pebbles and drink water.

'Have a little sleep now. We'll take a walk around later... if you want to,' he says.

When Horrible passes my cage, I growl at her, show my claws and teeth. I hope she's scared that I'll bite her.

Sleep is my escape until I hear his voice again.

'Come Pretty One, let's take a little walk.' He opens the

cage door. I follow, but I am still afraid – my belly close to the floor, my ears back and tail down. As we walk, passing the other cats in their cages, some call out to me. One hisses. The young Human strokes my head, and walks close to me.

'Don't worry about them,' he says. Uncertain once more, I stop to look up at him. 'Do you want to go back to your cage?' He asks. I allow him to carry me to my cage.

I rush into my basket to hide.

After a few days, I am more accustomed to my cage and the other cats. My walks are enjoyable. I run around the other cat's cages, and in the fenced garden. Back in my cage, I am engrossed in watching Handsome Male. He knows he is good to look at with his cute bum and lustrous fur coat of spots and stripes.

I count the days of my incarceration. This is day twelve. Will it never end? Will Karen ever come back for me?

At last, I hear her voice. She has returned from her holiday.
Cats Alive! About time too!

She talks to me, but I ignore her. I am placed in my carry box for the drive home with all the stopping and starting. The door of my box opens. I am home in my territory again.

'Welcome home Bella,' she says in her sweetest voice.

Though I desperately want to go to her, smell her and feel her hands touching me, I cannot. I hurt too much inside. Filled with conflicted emotions, I run and hide.

'What's the matter, Treasure? You know how much I love you, and that I wouldn't ever leave you there.'

She calls me several times. Eventually I go to her with faltering steps. I lie on my back exposing my tummy, expressing my hurt. As she is about to touch me, I feel the hurt again, and I sit up. Then she is on the carpet next to me holding out her hand. Slowly, I rub my head against it, and allow her to stroke me.

I leave her. Now, I have the extremely important task of examining my territory. I check the entire house to ensure that all is safe – as I left it. In the kitchen, she opens a tin – a mix of tuna and chicken. I can't resist it. Soon the food is gone. I clean my mouth with my paws.

The period away from my territory and Karen was awful, even though the nice Human tried to help me. I adapted to life in the cattery, but it drained me emotionally. Right now, I no longer love Karen unconditionally. I am too afraid of losing her. She will have to prove herself worthy of my love and trust all over again. I watch her every move. I follow her and sleep lightly. Will she stay with me or leave me again? Can I trust her love? If she goes out, I wait for her at the front door. At night, I lie so close to her that our breaths mingle. She is mine, and filled with Cat Love, I dare not let her go. In her sleep, she pats my head.

A few days later, I recover my Catness, but I am not the same naive cat. I realise that anything could happen to disturb my security.

The air is cool inside the house. Outside the wind bites. While I was away most of the leaves fell from the trees.

Karen and Tony sit close to each other as they watch television, and talk. Their holiday seems to have helped them, even if it did nothing positive for me. The room is full of loving feelings. When Karen and Tony are happy, Karen has less time for me. I have to get used to it, I tell myself.

At least the atmosphere in the house is joyful again.

When it is time for a long sleep during the night, I begin my sleep rituals. They are specific, important rituals based on our distant Cat Past when we were vulnerable to predators. Indulged, domestic cats no longer need the rituals, but they are part of us and seem wired into our brains. Stray cats without secure homes revert to these rituals, and need them to stay alive. Rituals reinforce Catness – our security and survival. I regularly change the places where I sleep at night, choosing from several spots. It is dangerous to be too predictable and defenceless when asleep. I eat and drink facing the door. Food could distract me. I need to be vigilant – aware of any enemies. I take no chances. Before a long sleep, I circle my sleeping place several times to ensure it is safe. I watch new Humans carefully too, before approaching them.

During the early hours, I patrol the entire house, check that Karen is safe in her bed next to Tony, and jump onto her side of the bed.

I know that Karen understands cats, and me in particular, but I doubt she understands the reasons for some of my rituals that make her laugh.

It has been a few weeks since Dane has visited Karen. I am happy to see him again. He is not holding onto his mother this time, and runs into the room to greet me.

'Hello, Bella. I missed you so much.' His hands and arms are tightly wound around me, cuddling, nuzzling and kissing. I rub his hand with my cheek. Finally he lets go, thank goodness, and I nestle in his small arms.

'How are you Dane?' Karen asks.

'I'm so happy. Mum and dad say that I can have a puppy.'

'We hope that a puppy will help Dane,' his mother says.

While Dane's mother and Karen talk, he hugs me and begins to cry.

As much as I dislike hugs, I put my paws around him.

Slowly, and in a soft voice, he tells me about the fire in the house next door. I feel sleepy as he tells me his long story. I miss a lot of what he is saying, but I stay close to him. Somehow, I know it is important for him to think I am listening. That is my job, my purpose, I tell myself.

I try to stay awake, but by the time Dane leaves with his mother, I am asleep.

'Dane left feeling much happier, Bella. You are an excellent therapist,' Karen says, as she gives my head a pat. 'You are getting better at it all the time. I love you!'

After being in the cattery with many other cats, the house seems quiet. Outside the grass and leaves in my garden have withered, but Karen has remembered to plant sufficient catnip, and it grows in abundance.

I am bored, lonely and restless. There are fewer mice and rats in my garden now, but I run around to exercise and pretend I am chasing them. Though I play with Karen most days, it is not enough for me. The cats that come past my high fence to chat can't even join me in my garden, but I wish they could.

In trying to keep me safe, Karen had isolated me.

At last, she notices that the brown cat living with our back neighbours comes to visit me regularly at the fence. Before allowing her to join me in my garden, she asks the neighbours if their cat has had its vaccinations. The brown cat must be safe because Karen opens the gate in the fence to let her in.

Slowly Brown Cat enters. Without taking her eyes off

me, she moves towards me. We sniff each other as we step cautiously around each other. She checks my territory. Once she feels satisfied she is safe, we begin to play. After all our exertion, we sleep in the weak sunlight.

When Karen doesn't need me, I call her to open the gate for Brown Cat. There are other cats that prowl as well. Karen calls them feral and refuses to allow them into the garden. Dogs of all sorts come past the fence barking and growling, but I ignore them.

Honey, a tiny dog slightly smaller than me with a fluffy coat, lives with the Humans on the other side of my garden. She sits and barks at the gate between her garden and mine every day. Karen says she is a Toy Pom.

For such a tiny creature, her mouth is large and her jaw looks strong. As we do not speak the same language, we find each other confusing.

Her bark is loud and sharp. Instead of growling at me like some of the bigger dogs, she whines. What an unpleasant wailing sound. I haven't heard a dog sound like that before. It might mean she is upset or want something. Perhaps a dog's wailing is similar to a cat's meow. I am learning that when dogs wag their tails they are happy, or excited in a positive way. They are nothing like us. Dog language is strange, almost as strange as human language.

Our tails express so many of our emotions. Humans who know and like cats understand how important our tails are in showing our feelings. A wildly flicking cat's tail means annoyance or anger, even boredom. A tail held high with a question mark at the tip can signal a playful or loving mood. I am sure that Honey has trouble understanding my tail.

Today Honey is scratching the fence wire, whining and her tail is wagging. I think she wants to come into my garden to play. Honey's owner calls her, but she continues to sit at the fence watching me. As small as she is, she knows what she wants, unlike most dogs who seem to follow each other or their owner.

Her owner laughs. 'Leave Bella alone, you silly doggie. She's a cat. Dogs and cats do not get along. You are both predators – always have been. If you had grown up together as babies it might have been different.'

Today, Karen opens the gate for Honey. Karen and the Humans next door must have talked.

'Take it slowly, Honey. You don't need to get your face scratched,' her owner says, but Honey races into the garden.

She is not as cautious a cat.

Racing Rats! My body arches. My tail stands erect and bristles like one of the brushes in the cupboard, and I hiss at her. She is not intimidated. She sits and waits, her head to the side as if trying to fathom my message.

There will be no further communication from me. I want nothing to do with this little dog.

I ignore her. She jumps and barks. What a dominant little creature. As soon as she comes closer, I climb up the half-tree and observe her. She scratches the base of the tree, and barks endlessly.

The Ancient Cat Voice in my head says, dogs are not to be trusted – not Honey or any dog, even one as tiny as her.

While I eye her, I sharpen my claws on the bark of a branch. My sharpened claws are my best weapon. Karen cut the tips of my claws but they are still lethal. Obviously, Honey has no clue about cats – an advantage for me. I will make sure that she will have a very long wait.

It is a breezy day and her canine scent floats up to me. Her fur is filthy and she stinks. Her owner ought to wash her. Cats are so clean, as we wash ourselves often. Unless we are sick, we do not smell. That's why Humans enjoy having us on their beds. Imagine that filthy bundle on a bed. Meeyuk!

Honey is extremely annoyed, and tired of waiting for me. She paces and growls, showing her teeth. She attacks the tree trunk instead of me and barks again.

She can scratch all she likes, but she can't climb. I leap onto the roof of the house. Up there I am even safer.

Dogs don't belong in my garden. As for playing with her... it won't happen.

I've had enough of Honey. *Meow, Meow*! I call to Karen.

*Thank Cat's Nine Lives, a*t last she hears me.

'Where are you Precious?' She spots me on the roof.

I stare at her pleadingly.

This has been enough dog to fill the rest of my life.

Karen turns to her neighbour. 'I think it's time for Honey to go home.'

At last Honey's owner whistles for her. She responds immediately, and leaves.

'Your cat and Honey don't get along together. It is a waste of time. She won't be back,' the neighbour says.

What in Catland! Stupid Honey is at the fence again today, but she looks different. She is prancing and showing off her clean coat, a fluff ball, shades lighter. She's had a bath and smells of flowers. What a huge improvement! I go closer, and somehow our noses almost touch through the fence wire. I step back quickly.

I would prefer to like her, but she is a dog and I don't trust her.

I hover for a moment undecidedly and then walk away.

Karen is calling, 'Come, Bella, Tamara is not doing well, and we must visit her at the hospital.'

After my usual resistance, my harness is on, and I am in

the carry box as we drive to the hospital. We park, and then Karen carries me through the hospital to Tamara's ward. Her parents and brother are sitting next to her bed looking gloomy.

'Thank you for coming, Tamara has been asking to see Bella,' her brother says.

Karen lifts me out of my carry box and places me on Tamara's bed.

'There you are, my darling, Bella's here now,' Tamara's mother says lovingly.

Tamara is weaker and paler today, and her head has no hair. She talks softly, but I hear her say, 'I need a huge cuddle, Bella.'

Purring loudly, I move up higher and put my paw on her shoulder. She is very ill and I can tell that she will be going away soon, but I hope to make her passing easier. I nestle closer.

Tamara strokes me slowly, touching my fur with the tips of her fingers. She makes sure to caress my cheeks, tickle my chin and neck.

She wants me to remember this delightful experience... to remember her. I sense the inner beauty of her being, and know that I will not forget her.

Karen is about to place me in my carry box and leave, when a doctor stops us.

'Could you bring your cat to visit a young patient who adores animals? A few minutes with your cat will lift his spirits.'

I rub my head against Tamara. She strokes me lovingly, and gives me a long look that says "goodbye".

Then Karen clips on my lead and we follow the doctor to a skinny teenager who is watching television.

'Benjamin, this is Karen and her cat Bella. They've come for a quick visit,' the doctor says.

'Wow! What a great surprise! I love cats,' he says, opening his arms to me.

'You can go onto the bed,' Karen says to me.

I jump into the boy's arms and he holds me tight, but I do not squirm. He is sick and needs to feel my *Cat Love*.

As he strokes me, he asks Karen about me.

I delight in listening to Karen talk about me.

'This visit from Bella has been the best thing that has happened to me all day. Please, visit me again if you are in the hospital.'

I enjoyed being with him and hope to see him again.

Once we are home, Karen strokes me, kisses my head, and tells me how much she loves me. I am filled with love for her too.

Cat Delight! Late that afternoon, while Karen is working, I am on her pillow! It is here that I drift into another one of my important dreams.

The night sky is dark apart from a milky moon. I am in a dense forest, on a high branch of a tall tree. I listen to wild dogs howling. Like their wolf ancestors, the dogs are talking to each other. At a lower pitch we cats chatter, sharing warnings about the danger of dogs in the forest. If the dogs detect the slightest movement in the trees or smell the presence of cats, they will hunt for us in packs. Their sense of smell is even more powerful than ours. They are huge, fast animals with strong jaws and sharp teeth, and present a serious challenge.

At sunlight, dead cats, rabbits, possums, and other small animals litter the forest floor. I am hungry, but I hide and wait until the sun is blazing and the dogs are asleep, before hunting for mice or crawling creatures. I am a lone, stealthy hunter, and I do not go hungry. I catch a mouse and eat it immediately.

I wake from my dream, yawn and stretch. I am hungry but it is not dinnertime yet.

The night is still, the moon has vanished and the sky is streaked with yellow and green.

Major Cat Alert! My whiskers flutter, my nose quivers. I sense a huge change is on its way in Catland.

I wake early. Restlessly, I patrol my house and do my *Cat Work* of rubbing my scent on the furniture and carpets to mark my territory. Outside, I leave my mark on the plants and fence, and pee on the rocks to reinforce my ownership.

The cold wind blows dry leaves and twigs in my face as I pace along the fence, listening. I have prepared for whatever is about to happen. I find a protected spot, curl up for warmth and sleep lightly.

Later, I am in the garden, in the pale sunlight, when the heavy, crunching sound of human footsteps alerts me. A tall, foul smelling Human walks along my fence carrying a box.

When he sees me, he laughs. His laugh is not like Karen's happy laugh. 'The people who live here are stupid cat lovers. I think I've found the ideal place,' I hear him muttering to himself. 'Perfect for this strange looking creature with big ears. It must be the ugliest kitten I have ever seen.'

He laughs again, looks about, checking that no one except me sees him. Then he tries the gate into my special garden. It is open. Karen forgot to lock it. He places the box on the grass, makes certain no one has spotted him, and disappears.

I have a sense of dread in my tummy. I listen and sniff. There is something alive in the box. Slowly I approach it. I hear a thin, soft *mew, mew,* the sound of a distressed kitten calling for help. The box is closed, but I claw at it until I open it. Inside is a tiny, skinny kitten.

Purrrr, pree, purrrr Little One, I say to it softly, as I grip it in my mouth and lift it out of the box. I place it gently on the grass. It looks exhausted and terrified.

'Don't be afraid, I'll look after you,' I tell it.

Quickly, I carry it in my mouth through my cat door into the house. The small thing is barely hanging on to life. I leave the kitten on the kitchen floor, search for Karen and call loudly for her.

'What's worrying you, Bella?' She asks, following me as I race ahead of her to the kitchen.

She sees the kitten. 'Poor, little darling, you're alive, but weak and cold. I'll give you something to eat and keep you warm.'

She grabs a towel and wraps the kitten in it. Then she puts some of my special cat milk and food into the whirring machine.

'You are even too weak to eat. I'll look for something to help you,' she says.

She takes a clear bag from the cupboard and cuts a small hole in its corner. She fills the bag with some of the mixed food. While holding the kitten wrapped in the towel, she feeds him slowly from the bag through the cut corner. Slowly, he sucks the food from the bag.

Thank Cats! I watch amazed. Karen is a Cat Mama. She most definitely had to be a cat in her last life. Now I am convinced. How does she know how to feed him? She hasn't even carried and suckled her own human kitten yet.

He rests, and is a little stronger after the food. She places him on the floor. Though he is slightly unsteady, he manages to stand. The remainder of the food she pours into a small bowl so that he can feed himself. While he eats, she puts down a saucer of water for him. Then she makes him a warm temporary basket and a litterbox.

'I know that you won't want to share litterboxes,' she says to me.

When he has finished most of his food, she takes him to his litterbox, hoping he knows how to use it. I'm surprised that he does.

'Someone must've known we owned a cat and wanted us to look after you,' she says, as she looks closely at him. 'You're filthy, and if you're going to stay here for even a short while, I will have to clean you.'

The word "clean" sends shivers all the way down to the tip of my tail. Cleaning, like washing can be a terrible experience.

'I'm sorry Sweetheart, she says, as she takes a wet cloth and tries to wipe the kitten, but he squirms and cries.

There must be two cats inside my head telling me different things. The one cat says that I should growl and hiss at the kitten so that Karen sends him away, as he is going to bring me a lot of trouble. This is my house and I do not want company. The other kinder cat tells me that I tried to save him, and now I can help to lick him clean like his mama would. I listen to the kind cat in my head and I lick the kitten all over.

He purrs for the first time, and I look at him. He has eyes the colour of a clear, blue sky, a soft, white body, but his feet and big ears are the palest brown. As tiny as he is, I know that he is a very different kind of cat to me and my mama. Even his *mew, mew* is different. I have not seen or heard a cat like him before, and I cannot stop myself wondering if he has *Catness*, the blood of a real, strong cat inside him.

Karen is pleased with me for cleaning him, strokes my head and tells that I am 'her precious, a good girl.'

She stands back and looks at him. 'You are a lovely little creature. I want to keep you, our second found cat...so I hope Tony won't argue. I hope too that Bella won't mind you being here, even though she was here first, and the house is hers.'

Little Blue Eyes is terrified. He hides under a chair.

Enough of him! I'm not going to try to drag him out. He is safe from immediate danger. I have done my job. Now Karen and Tony can look after him. I am too tired. Time for a long sleep.

I wake to hear Tony shouting.

'What, another cat!' He says with a *hiss* in his voice when he sees the kitten.

After Karen explains how I found the exhausted kitten in the garden, he is kinder.

'He is a beauty and a pure bred Siamese, by the look of him. Why would someone dump him?'

'Siamese cats don't look like other cats. Their elongated bodies and markings are unusual, and they have huge ears as kittens. The person who left him here him might not have seen a cat like this before, and not wanted him. Maybe he didn't realise that the cat was worth selling, and could've fetched quite a large amount. Who knows, but let's keep him, anyway.' Karen says.

'Yes, it's our good fortune. We'll keep him,' Tony says.

'He can be your cat. Bella seems to be mine.'

Tony walks around before answering. 'I like the name Oliver. It suits him.'

'Oliver is his name, then,' Karen says, and gives Tony a hug and kiss.

'So Bella, Oliver is your new friend,' Karen says to me in her sweet voice. She bends to talk to the kitten. 'Bella will be kind to you, and teach you all you need to know... won't you Bella?'

As if I don't have enough to do, she is now given me the job of teaching him the ways of the house.

I turn from Oliver, Karen, and Tony, and walk away.

'We'd better keep the two cats separate while they get used to each other,' Tony says.

Karen puts Oliver in a room at the back of the house. It is the room where I stayed when Karen brought me home. He has his food and basket there, and his litterbox is in the room as well.

She leaves me and goes to Oliver. I realise she is trying to help him to become accustomed to his new home.

Rats! I miss her, and of course I'm jealous that he has all her attention. I must never, ever complain of being lonely or bored again!

Later, I sleep on her side of the big bed, and try to forget about the new kitten. Karen strokes me and tells me she loves me. After a few hours, she wakes and moves me out of the way.

'I have to go and feed Oliver now...see if he's alright,' she whispers.

I follow her slowly, hearing his distressed mewing at the back of the house. The kitten is trembling with fear. She feeds him and talks to him in a whisper.

The good cat in me, the Therapy Cat, goes to him. I slip into his basket and give him reassuring purrs. I tell myself that of course I won't be sleeping with this kitten permanently. I am helping him just this once.

The next morning he is stronger. He eats his food and goes to the litterbox before returning to his basket. I have done my job for now.

Life is good, unless I think of Oliver. I go past his room and listen at the closed door. At least he has stopped mewing.

I am confused and wish I could settle down. I am restless and unhappy. My food I leave half-eaten and my thoughts are constantly about change. Before he arrived, I called the house, my house, the garden was my garden, and Karen was all mine too. Everything was mine.

I know that I ought to be fair and kind to him, and that right now I am behaving like a Catyuk. I am a healer, a Purr Therapist for children and other Humans, and yet I am being horrid to this tiny, orphaned kitten. Of all cats, I should remember what being alone and unwanted feels like, and treat him with care.

But, I want things to be the way they were before he came. I hate changes in my routine. Part of me wants to scratch his beautiful, little, blue eyes and bite those big ears of his. I know it is all about my territory, my place as top cat and about Karen too. Instinct and love for her drives me. I am afraid he might steal Karen's love from me.

Eventually, I will have to learn to share it all, even though it will be extremely hard. He is still a tiny kitten, so I don't need to worry about sharing the house with him yet.

Karen is talking on the phone to Mia's mother. 'I'm so pleased that she's feeling stronger.' She laughs, 'I'm not surprised Mia wants to see Bella again soon...and tell her that we are both thrilled that she is recovering so well. She is welcome to visit Bella after school.'

After lunch, Karen makes a few calls on her hand phone. Then I lie next to her. While she is stroking me, and tickling my tummy, she says, 'Don't you think it's time for you and Oliver to live together in the house?'

Karen's questions are often demands.

Reluctantly, I follow her towards the back of the house, to Oliver's room. My tail hangs down, my ears are back. At that moment I am a nasty Meeyuk.

'Come on, Bella, hurry up!' She says.

Rats Tails! Surely I have done enough to help and comfort him.

Little Blue Eyes is in his basket. She leaves, and I am alone in the room with him. He stays in his basket, staring at me.

My grrrrrr is soft, but I need to remind him that I am the boss, the top cat, and that he should be wary of me and know he is in my territory, that I was here first.

Oliver's blue eyes search mine. The brave little one is trying to stand his ground, but he is nervous inside. Tentatively, he steps out of his basket, but he waits for me to make the first move. I sniff him, and then allow him to sniff me. I walk around the room and then leave.

He stays in his room most of the time. Sometimes, I hear him mewing when he is lost. If I hear his mews becoming louder, I run to his aid, and help him to find his way in the large house marked with my scent. He will eventually find his way through his own scent channels.

This morning, I tell myself that I am more used to him now. The time has come for me to help him to learn about the house. I have to make him part of life in the house or we will fight as he grows older. I have no choice.

Gradually, I encourage him to follow me through the rooms in the house, past every corner and piece of furniture marked with my scent. My smell is everywhere, but he leaves his mark occasionally.

Tony looks at Oliver lovingly. 'He has only been here for a few weeks and he's almost twice the size he was when Bella found him. The two cats are completely different. Bella is just a Tabby, but Oliver is a gorgeous, purebred Siamese. I still can't understand why he was given away.

The person who dumped him must've been crazy.'

So, I'm not good enough for Tony? Just a Tabby? I flick my tail against his leg three times and hope it stings. So what if Oliver is a Siamese, whatever that is! It's who a cat is inside that matters. It is their Catness.

Tony doesn't have Karen's understanding of cats. I am certain of that. Karen made me feel loved and beautiful from the day she found me. She calls me her special cat, and lets me know that Oliver will not change our close relationship. Whenever I am jealous of Oliver, I remember Karen's love and try to relax.

I wonder how long it will take for the two of us to bond. Other than being feline, and having a cat's features he is unlike me in many ways. Though he is still a kitten, I can tell he will be leaner and longer than me. His meow is sharper and louder than mine. He is far more talkative and very active. I can't remember being at all like him when I was that little.

Oliver taps me with his paw and runs ahead, asking me to play. *Fast Rats!* This little one can run. When I don't respond he bites my tail. Frustrated with him, I chase him away.

At first, Oliver refuses to go outside into the wet and cold, but I push him through the special door into the garden.

He must learn to go outside. He is cat, isn't he? He has to act like one. There are no flowers or leaves out there now, but he can run about and learn to catch creeping, furry things.

He is nervous at first and hides. He watches me, and slowly follows me to the fence, to the bare half-tree, the rocks and the bushes. He begins to run and enjoy himself. I catch a lizard, and play with it. Imitating me, he catches a worm, and throws it in the air.

We return to the house, I once called mine. When I jump onto my favourite chair, he stands and looks at me not knowing what to do.

Prrup prrup, I say to him, and he jumps up to join me. I touch his sleek, small body with my paw and he comes closer. We fall asleep together. When I wake, he is still asleep.

I lick his tiny face and feel true, caring warmth towards him for the first time.

He is behaving himself, but I know it won't last. His blue eyes have naughty shining in them. Soon my troubles with him will start.

When Dane and his mother arrive, both are smiling. The energy in the room is positive.

'Hello, Bella. I missed you.' His tiny hands touch me all over and he hugs me. Then he runs to Karen and hugs her too.

Excitedly, his words rush out. 'Karen, Karen, I have a puppy now. He is black, and his name is Misty.'

His mother says happily, 'Dane adores Misty. He feeds him and changes his water. He is helping me to train him too.'

A dog is better than nothing, but a poor substitute for a cat. The main thing is that Dane is happier.

'Show Karen a photo of your puppy,' Dane's mother says.

Karen smiles. 'He's very cute. I'm pleased for you Dane.'

Dane sits on the floor next to me, while Karen talks to his mother.

'I love my little Misty, but I love you too, Bella,' he says. 'I talk to Misty, but he's still young and runs about all the time. Not like you, Bella. You listen and understand.'

'Thank heavens Dane is much happier since we bought Misty for him, but he still has a few moments of crying and clinging to me...and he hardly talks about the fire next door,' his mother says.

Dane's smile disappears and his sad face is back.

I know he needs me, so I nuzzle against him.

Karen takes Dane's hand. 'Maybe now that you have told Bella why you are sad inside, you will be able to tell your Mum, Dad and me, how you feel about the fire.'

'I will have to tell Misty about it first. He doesn't know.'

'That's a good idea, Dane. Misty lives in your house and he knows nothing about what happened in the house next door. He will understand when you tell him about it, I'm sure,' Karen says.

Dane nods. 'Yes, I will tell Misty.'

Their talk becomes boring and I worry about Oliver scratching the carpets and furniture while we are busy.

When Dane and his mother are ready to leave, he pats my coat and kisses my head.

'Bye, bye, Bella...love you,' he says.

The wind howls, bare branches crackle and heaps of leaves block the special cat door leading into my garden. Inside the house, the windows rattle and cold creeps in from beneath the doors. I am sublimely warm next to one heating vent, while Oliver is near a vent of his own.

Karen calls me. Reluctantly, I leave the vent to join her in the therapy room.

'Mia and her mother will be here in a few minutes,' Karen says.

As the door to the therapy room opens, I run to greet Mia.

'Hello, Bella, I've missed you so much,' she says as she bends to stroke me. 'I'm back at school and feeling much better.'

I notice that she has grown taller and she looks stronger.

Her mother smiles broadly. 'Mia has recovered well and the doctors are pleased with her. She has changed a lot since you saw her last. She is happier at school, but she still lacks a little confidence. I'll let her tell you her news.'

'The bullies aren't worrying me as much now. The new friends I made love cats too, and we share cat stories. Before school, during recess, and after school we stick together. We ignore the bullies and feel safer.'

'That's great news, Mia.'

Mia's tells Karen more about her new friends, and then Karen asks, 'When are you going to play the violin for your class?'

'My teacher asked me to play, but I told her that the others in the class won't like my classical music.'

'That might be true,' Karen says. 'Maybe you could play some popular songs they know and like. They can join in by singing or clapping their hands.'

'I guess I could.'

'You haven't visited Bella after school yet,' Karen reminds her. 'You are welcome to spend time with her. In the afternoon, she is usually in the side garden unless it is raining. Open the gate and go in, but don't forget to close it when you leave.'

'I would love to play with Bella. I'll visit her tomorrow after school.'

I feel happy and look forward to her visit, but what about Oliver? Will he like Mia? It will work itself out, I guess.

Rats! How could I have complained I was lonely before he came? Now he is with me too much, or I worry about him and his antics.

Karen is waiting for me in the laundry. 'Come on, my sweetie...grooming time.'

It's cold in the laundry and I know that she wants to comb me with the skinny comb that hurts when I have knots in my fur.

'Hurry up Bella...I'm freezing waiting for you.'

I'm staying warm. She can wait.

'Fine. I'm coming to find you...and pick you up. I know that you don't like being carried.'

I give in, and go to the laundry for the hair combing torture.

'You're a wonderful Therapy Cat but such a "drama queen", she says, as she combs my coat. 'It's almost over. Now for the brush. You enjoy having your coat brushed.'

Brushing is invigorating and sensual. I hope she goes on and on. It stops and I shake myself. I feel fresh and clean. All my dry hairs have gone.

'Sorry...claws too,' she says, grabbing me.

Off go the tips of my sharp weapons.

Oh well, that's Catland.

I hear the garden gate open. It's Mia. She walks uncertainly. I run to her, circle her legs with my tail, and purr.

'Oh, Bella, It's lovely to see you,' she says stroking my head.

I am filled with Cat Love for this human child. She is starting to blossom and I'm thrilled.

We sit under the half-tree, and she pats me with love in her fingers. She has a gentle touch and I am in *Cat Heaven*.

'I brought you a toy to play with,' she says, with her hand in her pocket.

A bouncy thing slithers across the ground. She pulls it, and it is a snake. She dangles it, and it turns into a mouse. I try to catch it, but Mia makes sure it is too clever for me. It hops and hides, and hops again. Just when I think I have caught it, it's gone. We play a while longer, and at last I have it. I bite it, but it tastes awful. I will play with it again later.

She looks towards the gate. 'Mum is here for me. I'll see you soon, darling, Bella.'

She puts her hand into her other pocket and leaves another present for me on the grass. It is chicken, and I eat it quickly.

Next time she visits she will have to meet Oliver. She will adore him, I'm sure. I wanted one more afternoon alone with Mia before sharing her with Oliver.

Blue Eyes sits near the window making chattering noises as he looks outside.

He is restless. Something is bothering him lately, but I can't see or smell it. He is growing into a strong and muscular cat, but he is emotionally sensitive and becomes easily frustrated. I wonder if his unease is due to what Tony calls, his fine breeding. The house is quiet and nothing in the garden could distress him. I stopped the dog next door from barking. The fence prevents stray cats and dogs from entering our garden. Even my friend, Brown Cat, has not visited me since Oliver arrived. I wonder where she has gone. He is not restrained, and is free to roam throughout the house, except for the therapy room. He is well fed and loved. However, he reacts to the slightest changes in routine. If Karen is in a hurry or is tired, or the tone of her voice alters slightly, he runs away or turns his back on her. I doubt he has the temperament of a Therapy Cat.

By now, he has lost his kitten chubbiness, and I have to admit that he is extremely handsome. Not sensuously handsome like the Bengal in the cattery, but he is elegant. He is slim, long, and moves athletically, with newly acquired physical prowess. His silky white and cream body fur is magnificent. Once he is fully-grown, his brown, boot paws will be smaller, rounder and more delicate than mine. His eyes are his most striking feature – deep blue like the tiny, summer flowers in the garden. His face is balanced now. He has grown into his big pointed ears that dominated his face as kitten.

I tell myself that we are both felines, but he differs from me in so many ways that it remains a puzzle. I look at myself in the mirror and I am beautiful, as Karen and other people say, but my appearance is distinctly different to Oliver's.

He is starting to leave his marks on corners of the rooms and furniture near mine, creating his own scent path in the house. I have begun to allow him to make his own path, as long as he realises that he is still in my territory. When he becomes an adult, we will share the house. We are growing closer, chatting and lying next to each other for warmth. This is all positive.

Though Oliver goes to Karen, he is more Tony's cat than ever. It is obvious that Tony adores him. He pets him gently, and talks to him lovingly At night, when Tony is home, Oliver is in the television room next to him or curled up on his lap.

I consider myself the far luckier cat, having Karen's special love.

Emma, the young woman who was upset after breaking up with her boyfriend, Steve, is here to see Karen. She is dressed in black again, but today she smells fresh and her hair is neat. She smiles, and even stops at my basket to say, 'Hi Kitty.'

She tells Karen her news. 'My friends have been amazing. They supported me after Steve's friends posted nasty photos of me on the Internet. They found pictures where I look great, and posted them. There were hundreds of positive responses.'

I wish I understood the technological devices that Humans talk about. They are not in a cat's world...not yet, anyway.

'Lots of guys seem to like the way I look with some extra curves, but I can't see why.'

Karen smiles, and they discuss how people's tastes differ.

'Did you do any of the homework about the negative way you've been thinking about yourself?' Karen asks.

Karen is wearing her strong face. It means she is definite about something and won't shift or negotiate. I see it when she calls me, and wants me to come to her in a hurry.

Emma looks down and shakes her head. 'I've had so much going on that I didn't get around to it.'

Karen frowns and I know she is dissatisfied.

'Working on it will help you a lot, and make a big difference to the way you feel about yourself.'

'I understand more about the homework now. I'll find time for it,' Emma says.

Karen's homework seems to help many of the teenagers who visit her, but that is another thing I don't understand. As long as it makes them healthier and happier that is most important.

Anyway, it is a mystery to me that Humans can change the way they feel about themselves. Cats do not change their ideas about themselves. I am extremely pleased to be a cat, and I like myself the way I am.

Oliver is bored and restless this morning. Earlier he shredded the newspaper. Now his claws are into documents on Tony's desk. He tears at the papers, enjoying the sound of them ripping. Tony is not at all pleased that he cannot read his morning paper, but he controls any anger he has towards Oliver. He shakes the shreds of paper at Oliver, and says "no" loudly. But, when he goes into his study and finds his important documents in pieces, his fury erupts.

'You little devil! Don't you ever do this again,' he shouts, waggling his finger at Oliver.

It is the first time Tony has been so angry with him. Oliver runs to hide under the bed.

I doubt Tony's rage will stop Oliver. I knew that once he felt comfortable in the house he would be naughty.

Now that Tony has left for work, Oliver chases his tail. Then he turns somersaults on the carpet. Bored with that, he digs a hole in the soil of an indoor pot plant. Not satisfied yet, he stretches up the wall and his claws grasp a low painting. It crashes to the floor.

Enough!

I swat him with my paw.

'Do you think you are my mother telling me what to do? There are enough rules in this house without you interfering,' he says in his Siamese dialect. As if to prove to me that he can do whatever he likes, he shows off his skills by climbing the drapes.

Rat's Poo! Now he is hanging onto the curtain rail, but his claws are caught in the fine material.

Meow, meeow, meeeeow help me. I'm going to fall, he calls in panic.

'Sorry Oliver, but I'm too heavy to climb up there,' I say. 'I'll look for Karen.'

She hears his distress call, and runs out of the therapy room. When she sees him dangling from the rail, her face is angry. She rescues him and says 'no' loudly. Then she sprays him with water. I hear his yowls of distress.

I've had the water treatment only once, and it almost stole one of my nine lives. I am not surprised that Oliver doesn't like it! I smile to myself, not because I want Blue Eyes to suffer, but he needs to learn some self-control. I wasn't like that at his age. I liked to play and run, but I was quieter and gentler. He is behaving like a rebellious, male teenager, taking risks, testing his limits. I hear parents of human, male teens who visit Karen complain about the same thing.

All Cats Alive! A teenage Siamese cat!

I go into the cold garden to escape from Oliver's antics. I need calm and quiet.

Do I like Oliver? He is a lot of trouble now, but he'll be grown up soon, and then I'll be able to tell if he's a real friend.

This is the second week that sad teenagers have come to see Karen.

I sense their misery and consuming worry. How dreadful! I wish I could understand why some young people feel so empty inside, and why their spirits are in such pain. Cats try to handle their lives, even in the worst circumstances. I keep being reminded how different we are to Humans. I think of Oliver, left in a box barely alive, and how he clung to life and recovered.

What is this deep, sad sickness that infects so many Humans? And why do they have it? Catland must be nothing like Humanland. I wish the sad ones had Cat-like resilience.

Dane is here with his mother again. He has grown a little and is smiling. He runs to me, hugs and pats me.

He is going to be a loving Human when he grows up.

'How are you, Dane,' Karen asks,

'I am happy!' He says.

'That's wonderful! What's been happening?'

'I told Misty about the fire next door and he said it was okay to tell you, Karen, Mum, and Dad everything.'

'We have talked a lot about the fire...and he's sleeping well now,' his mother says.

Dane smiles broadly at his mother.

'Dane's dad took him next door to show him the burned ground, and where a new house is going to be built soon,' she says.

'Did you see new, green plant shoots coming up where the fire burned the ground?' Karen asks.

'Yes, and there were some pretty flowers too. There is grass growing over the black. A garden will come back again.'

Cat Thanks! Dane seems to be almost well now. He will make new friends and move on, just like we cats do. I doubt he will be back to see Karen again. I will miss him.

Oliver delights in the way catnip affects him. He is in the garden nibbling what is left of the catnip. I hope Karen plants more when the sunshine is back.

Now he is running through the house to burn up his excess energy.

'I feel closed in, like a prisoner in here,' he says. 'There are too may rules in this house. I can't even make a noise when Karen is busy, and I have to behave in the television room. I need to live a little, experiment, and see the world outside before I grow up.'

'I understand, Oliver.' I say kindly. 'I felt the same, wanting to roam, see new places, but when I thought of how Karen saved my life and what a wonderful home I have here, I stopped myself.'

'I know Karen saved me too, and I am grateful. Tony is the best owner I could wish for, but I have something restless inside that makes me want to explore.'

Cats Above! I knew it. Tony's blue-eyed cat will give us

plenty of trouble before he grows up. It is becoming clearer to me each day that in many ways he is like the dissatisfied, human teenagers who come to seek help from Karen.

Mia is opening the gate to the garden. She has not met Oliver yet. I leave her to look around our dry garden, while I look for him in the house. He is asleep on the couch. When I wake him, he complains loudly. He stretches slowly and makes me wait by cleaning his face with his paw, before reluctantly following me into the garden. He blinks in the bright light.

Mia rushes towards Oliver.

'Oh, what an adorable new kitten! Aren't you magnificent, a beauty,' she says stroking his head.

It is silly, but I can't help it. I am jealous of Oliver. Everyone thinks he is so good looking and they have stopped telling me that I am beautiful.

'You must have a big job looking after him,' she says to me.

I turn away and flick my right whiskers in dissatisfaction. I have developed a habit of whisker flicking since Oliver arrived. Mia realises that I am jealous. Somehow, she manages to pet us both and talk to us lovingly.

Suddenly, a high-pitched bark disturbs us. Honey is running along her side of the fence and barking frenetically. Our voices probably alerted her. I ignore Honey's barking while Mia continues to stroke me. The pleasure of her touch distracts me, but Oliver races towards the fence and to Honey. I hear a twang of wire, as Honey tries to push her paw through a space in the fence.

Meeeow, Meeeow, I call to Oliver, but he ignores me. Fascinated by the tiny dog, he tries to squeeze under the gate towards her. I grab him by his scruff and smack his nose with my paw like mama smacked mine. I try to tell him that she is a dog with a powerful jaw, and that she will delight in biting him.

His *grrrrrrr* is loud and he almost attacks me. Honey leaves and Oliver turns his back on me, and then runs inside.

He is furious with me, but I don't care. He is still a kitten and has no experience of dogs. I will have to watch him in the garden in future. Honey may mean him no harm, but I am not sure, and I am vigilant. Oliver is annoyed now, but when he is older, he can fend for himself.

Caring for our young is another important aspect of Catness that I cannot avoid.

'Wake up, sleepy cat,' Karen says to me, as she rushes towards the kitchen. 'We are visiting the hospital today. We have two people to call on, Helena and Emma's friend, Ava. You had better eat your breakfast now, Bella, or you'll vomit in the car.'

I stretch, roll on the carpet, and slowly follow her to the kitchen. In the early morning, the house is dark and cold. Rain is thumping on the roof.

Rat's! It is not a day to go anywhere!

Karen has already filled my bowl with my food pebbles. She makes coffee and toast for herself. At the same time, she tidies and prepares breakfast for Tony. As she waits for her toast, she hurriedly dries dishes.

With all she is attempting to do at once, something will happen. I am waiting for it. Cats do one thing at a time, and well. We don't rush.

A cup slips out of her hand and smashes on the floor.

'Out of the kitchen, Bella, or you will cut yourself!' She says in a panicky voice.

She grabs the buzz machine to suck up the sharp, tiny pieces. The floor is safe again and I can eat my breakfast. As I eat, enjoying each mouthful, I watch her gulp down her small breakfast. When she finishes it, she holds her tummy in pain and moans. She swallows a white tablet with some water.

'Come on, Bella, we'll be late.'

She has my harness, lead and carry box ready. I am used to the harness now and find it less cumbersome. The distance we travel is further than usual, and in the early morning traffic the car constantly stops and starts. Just as well there was no time for a fuller breakfast. Finally we arrive. The unusual fragrance of the flowering trees and smell of the ground tell me that we are at a hospital we have not visited before.

As we pass through the doors, a Human stops us. He wants to know why Karen is bringing a cat into the hospital, and where she wants to take me. There is a long discussion and more Humans arrive. Karen produces papers from her bag, and we are on our way again.

This must be an enormous hospital because we walk a long distance, and then go into a small moving space that Karen calls a "lift". Karen stops to ask for directions and we walk further. As we approach Helena's ward, I smell a familiar odour. Dog.

Meow, meow I cry softly.

'Calm down, Bella! We are passing a blind man with his seeing eye dog,' she says.

I am confused.

A Human who helps at the hospital stops to talk to Karen.

'I hope your cat isn't afraid of the dog. He is a Therapy Dog, and is name is Roger. He has been trained not to attack cats or other animals. He is here often with his owner. Your cat has nothing to fear. These dogs are incredible. They are the eyes of their blind owners, and help them to attend appointments at the hospital, to cross roads, and go to places like the bank. They are loving companions too, and I don't know what blind people would do without them.'

I watch the blind man and his dog walk away.

'Is your cat a Therapy Cat?' The helper asks.

'Yes, and an excellent one, too.'

'We have Therapy Dogs and Cats at this hospital. Both do a great job of calming sick people and giving them affection.'

'Are you okay now, Bella?' Karen asks. 'There are many ways that dogs help people and do valuable work. Dogs and their owners have a strong bond. It is different to a cat's connection with an owner.'

Cat Knowledge! Learning about dogs to help blind Humans and dog therapists gives me a jolt. The discovery that there is a positive, caring side to the very creatures that make my life a misery, occupies my mind all along the winding passage to Helena's ward. That dogs perform a similar job to mine as therapists is incredible. There have to be some likeable, caring dogs. Perhaps I will meet a dog that I am not afraid of one day.

'We're here...at last!' Karen says, relieved.

But, we are stopped again, when a nurse asks loudly, 'Do you have permission to bring that animal into the ward?'

Karen explains that I am a certified Cat Therapist. We wait, and the nurse asks us to follow her. Helena is sitting in an large armchair and looking much healthier. Karen opens my carry box and lifts me onto Helena's lap.

'Ah, Karen, so good to see you...and Bella, my lovely friend. I'm so pleased you've come!'

I am pleased to see her too, and purr.

Helena strokes me, while she explains to Karen that she will be in hospital for about a week for tests, and to try new medication.

'Bella, when you visited me at home your purr and love

gave me hope. You have a unique healing gift.'

'Purrs are healing,' Karen says to Helena.

'They certainly help me,' she says, while kissing the top of my head.

Humans do such a lot of kissing. Surely touching noses or a cheek rub is enough.

There are eight other sick Humans in the ward and they all notice me.

'Puss, Puss, come to me,' each calls

'Okay, take the cat to them all, but not to the man in the corner bed. He's too weak to risk picking up an infection from an animal,' the nurse says.

Karen clips on my lead and I follow her to the sick Humans calling for me. They all want to pet me and cuddle. I purr for them all.

Three young doctors learn that I am visiting and rush up to us. 'Look who's here...a Therapy Cat,' one says.

They take turns in lifting me up, stroking me, and making comments.

'Isn't she a pretty cat and such lovely, kind eyes,' one says.

'So good natured too,' another adds.

I know all of this, and I will come again if Karen brings me. More important – I am hungry.

At last, a nurse finds some food for me and I eat it quickly.

Just as well, considering my small breakfast!

Karen leads me back to Helena. I jump onto her lap for a last cuddle.

'Our patients love you, Bella! Please visit us again,' one of the doctors says.

'I'll bring Bella again, soon,' Karen replies.

I'm inundated with attention and I like it. This is a lovely hospital!

We are back in a lift smelling powerfully of Humans.

'Now, we have to find Ava,' Karen says.

This time, a pleasant nurse helps us to locate Ava's bed. Ava looks pale and ill.

'Hi Ava, I'm Karen and I've brought my cat, Bella, to visit you. Your friend Emma told me how much you like cats, and asked me to bring her.'

Ava tries to sit up, but she is too weak. She falls back onto her pillow.

'That's amazing,' she says in a soft, low voice. 'I adore cats and Emma knows it. Thanks so much for coming!'

'I'm Greta, Ava's mother,' a woman sitting on a chair next to the bed says. 'Ava's had a terrible time. Someone spiked her drink at a party and it caused a serious allergic reaction. The paramedics came just in time. Thanks to them, she is still with us.'

I don't understand what made Ava so sick, but I know she is in need of purrs and cuddles.

The nurse offers to bring a towel, so that I can sit on the bed next to Ava.

'Maybe you'll cheer her up...and hopefully she'll eat,' the nurse says.

With my lead still on, Karen lifts me onto Ava's bed. I go to the pale hand searching for me. She pats my head, tickles me under my chin and behind my ears with an expert touch.

'Your fur is thick like my cat Lulu's. Come closer.'

I move up so Ava can cuddle me.

'What a cute, darling cat! I am so pleased you've come. Emma knows I'm crazy about cats.'

She is definitely a cat lover. I am pleased we are visiting her.

As I lie next to her, a tray with food arrives.

'Ava, you must eat if you want to feel better,' the nurse says. 'I've brought something for the cat too.'

'I'm not hungry,' Ava says emphatically and turns her head away.

Ava has to eat or she won't survive.

I stare at her without blinking, and place my paw firmly on her arm. I tap her lightly.

'Oh, alright Bella, we'll both eat then,' Ava says.

I jump down from the bed into Karen's arms, while a saucer of food for me appears on the floor.

I am in luck...more food. Tasty fish this time.

At first, Ava nibbles her food, and then she seems to grow hungrier and eats half of it. Once she has eaten, she is tired and her eyes begin to close. She gives me a goodbye pat before we leave.

Karen is awake as soon as light enters the house. I follow her to the kitchen. She leaves me food, but has no time for cuddles. She cuts thin slices of bread, places food from the fridge on the slices, and fills platters with fruit. Big and small cakes are already on the large table in the dining room.

Visitors must be coming.

She wakes Tony. After complaining, he helps by carrying cups and saucers, bottles and glasses into the room.

'We'll have to put the cats into their garden,' he says.

Before I have time to run and hide, Karen lifts me up and gently pushes me through the cat door into our garden. Tony grabs Oliver. She gives us food and water. Then she locks the little door so that we can't return to the house.

I stand at our cat door and listen.

I hear her telling Tony. 'It's cool and clear – a lovely day for the cricket match! There was no rain overnight, so the field next to the house should be dry.'

'I'm pretty sure our office team will show the bank employees how to play the game,' he replies with a laugh.

'It will be great fun.'

Cricket! Whatever is it? They are going to a lot of trouble to organise it.

Oliver and I are cold, and eventually find a spot in the early sunlight. From our garden, we hear noise in the house as Humans arrive. Soon the field next to us is dotted with Humans dressed in white. Until I become bored, I watch the little ball as it is flies, is hit, and is caught. Oliver, active as usual, tries to climb out of our enclosure to chase the ball, but I stop him. Instead, he sits on a branch of the half-tree and watches the game.

I wish the game would end, but it goes on for ages and ages. I try hard, but I do not understand it at all.

When they take a break for lunch, two men who own cats visit us in our garden. They make a fuss of us both, and feed us treats from inside the house. Then a third man joins them. I sniff him, and sniff again.

His left leg smells awful. I am certain that he is sick, but he is happy and laughing. He probably feels no pain and is unaware of his sickness.

I go to him and call *meow, meow* as loudly as I can, and point to his left leg with my nose.

'Has your cat gone crazy?' He asks Karen.

'I doubt it,' she replies.

I go to him again, call out, and once more I point to his left leg.

'She might be trying to tell you something', Karen says. 'Do you have any pain in that leg of yours?'

'Actually, my thigh hurts a bit, but I've put off going to the doctor.'

'Perhaps you should see your doctor,' Karen says. 'Bella is trying to give you a message.'

The man laughs about the idea that a cat could be giving him a message. The men return to the field to play their silly game. Oliver and I eat and then sleep.

Tony's gleeful shout wakes us, 'We've won...again!

The sun is asleep by the time Karen opens our door to let us into the house. I am cold and tired by now, and go to the big bed to sleep.

I dream I am a huge, powerful cat, a leader. I am on the tall mountain, I usually visit, looking down on acres of desert. Around me are smaller cats like me. They are hungry, and call out for food. There has been almost no rain. Food is scarce. On the peak of an opposite mountain, I distinguish another large, cat leader surrounded by smaller cats. He is mainly white with brown boots. His blue eyes stare defiantly. Both our ears are back, and our claws are sharp, ready for attack. His cats are hungry too. With insufficient food for both groups, it will be a fight for survival. The blue-eyed cat leaps off his mountain towards me.

I wake in fear as I recognise Oliver as my opponent. What a frightening dream! It is a warning. He could be a threat if I allow him to be one.

Winter

Our garden is bare. The last dry leaves have blown away in the wind and soon it will be too cold to play outside. I climb the half-tree. From my vantage point I can see the empty gardens of houses around us. The Humans and their animals are all indoors seeking warmth.

A noise at the gate alerts me. It is Mia. Pleased to see her, I rush to greet her. She is dressed in a coat, hat and gloves.

'It's a very cold day, but I didn't want to miss seeing you, Bella.'

Oliver is asleep on the couch and I don't wake him. I want Mia for myself again. We play with a ball and run in the garden until we are warm and tired.

I hear a rustle at the fence. A large black tom cat is pacing. He hisses at me and arches his back.

'Ooooh, he's a bully,' Mia says, looking concerned.

I stand erect, stare at him and hiss, and then turn my back on him.

He walks away.

A fight isn't necessary. All I did was stand up to him.

Mia laughs. 'That's how to treat bullies, Bella!'

When I am not working with Karen, I sit in my favourite spot on a heating vent. From here, I can see out of the window onto the bald grass, leafless trees, or watch the rain.

Oliver is six months old now. He enjoys being in the wet, cold garden, hunting for mice. When he comes inside, he shakes his coat and sits near a vent to warm up.

After a long sleep, I call Oliver, but he does not reply. Then I search every room and all his favourite hiding places. I force myself to go into the cold garden to search for him, but there is no sign of him. Half way along the wire fence, there is a heap of earth. Oliver must've been digging. After a closer look at the fence near the mound of earth, I notice a hole wide enough for a slim cat to pass through.

What in Catland is he up to?

The hole is too narrow for me, but he could've slipped through it easily. I call out for him again. No reply. I call and wait for him in the cold, but he does not come home. Frozen, I return to my heating vent and wait for Karen to emerge from the therapy room. She seems to take ages.

Meeeeow! Meeeeeeeeeeow! I call. I run to Oliver's usual spot at the vent, to show her that he has gone. She calls him too, searches the house, and then as I did, goes outside to look for him. I follow her, show her the hole in the fence and the heap of earth.

'The little devil has run away.' Her voice is both worried and angry.

'Oliver, come! Oliver!' She calls again, but he does not come. She waits, and calls again and again. She goes into the street to look for him, and visits the neighbours. No one has seen him.

When Tony arrives he's upset about Oliver's disappearance. In the dark, he searches and calls for Oliver.

'He'll come home,' he says, hopefully. But, the following day, Oliver does not come home and the house is too quiet.

Sad Rats! I have to admit that I am missing Oliver. I am fonder of him than I thought. Where could he be, and in this cold weather? I hope that nothing awful has happened to him – that he hasn't hurt himself, or been in a fight.

I think of his restlessness, due to being held captive, as he put it. Most of the time he managed to balance his frustration – his gratitude to Karen and Tony for the loving home and food they provided with his desire to wander, prey on smaller creatures, attack and dominate. His need to be wild and free appears to have asserted itself, and won. For a while, scratching his pole, chasing mice and insects in the garden was satisfying, but it was not sufficient.

At Oliver's age, I wanted to escape too. Not to hunt and dominate, but to mate and have kittens. Though I called to males who stalked the fence, they could not reach me. Then Karen took me to the vet to be neutered. It is not something I want to think about, as it upsets me too much.

Tony leaves the cat door open in case Oliver comes home. He goes to the tiny door every few hours hoping to see Oliver coming through it.

He is so distressed that he talks to me for the first time. 'Where is the little devil, Bella? I miss him so much!'

Tony's brief discussion with me, the first ever, surprises me so much that I go back into the garden. I call for Oliver again as loudly as I can, but I doubt he can hear me.

Stinking Fat Rats! Where are you, Oliver?

Karen is concerned that he has sufficient to eat and is warm enough.

'A few days ago, I was at the point of trimming the tips of his claws to stop him climbing the curtains, but I'm glad I didn't,' she says. 'He needs his sharp claws to survive out there.'

Another day passes, and another, and no Oliver. Tony looks miserable and avoids mentioning Oliver's name. The intensity of his love for Little Blue Eyes surprises me. I listen out for Oliver, but I have stopped calling for him. Though I do not want to accept that he has disappeared from my life, I hope he is alive and well. With him gone and the Brown Cat no longer visiting, I am lonely and a little sad.

Karen notices that I am unhappy. 'I can tell you're worried about Oliver. Sit in the therapy room with me,' she suggests.

Being with her gives me reassurance and I stop thinking

of all the awful things that could've happened to Oliver. My unhappy mood passes soon. It is replaced with anger. At least he could've told me he was leaving, and not just run off while I was asleep. Perhaps he didn't care if I worried about him.

Just as well we cats remains miserable for only a short while, Catness, our instinct to survive reawakens, and we continue. We are vulnerable but strong. We know that our lives are brief. Most wild cats live very short lives. At least indoor cats usually live longer. I appreciate each day and forget about Oliver.

Karen is preparing food in the kitchen and Tony is in his study working.

Cat Alert! Suddenly I hear scratching from outside the cat door. It doesn't sound like a rat or possum. Could it be Oliver? I listen and recognise his *meow.*

All the Cats in Catland! Little Blue Eyes is back! He's home with us! I run to Karen, then Tony and stand at the cat door meowing. Tony had closed the door, thinking that Oliver wouldn't return. Tony hears my call first and runs to open the door.

Oliver races into the house. He's skinny and filthy!

'Oliver's back,' Tony shouts excitedly.

Karen runs to see him. They are thrilled he is back, but he is too smelly to cuddle.

He is so thin that his bones protrude.

'You look as if you've been starving. You'll need feeding up. First some food,' she says, as she opens a tin of food for him.

He gulps down the food and asks for more.

She opens another tin but gives him the food slowly – one teaspoon at a time.

'Easy does it. If you eat too quickly you will vomit.'

After he's eaten, she calls him. 'It is a cold night, but I will have to bath you, Oliver. You're dirty and I have no option,' Karen says.

I hear the water running in the laundry and hide, in the event that Karen decides to give me a bath too. The last one I had in the warmer, summer weather was disgusting. I watch from behind the curtain as she grabs Oliver by the scruff of his neck like dirty washing, and puts him into the tub of soapy water. He begins to yowl, and a Siamese cat's yowl is dreadful. I heard him yowl once, when Karen squirted him with water. Hopefully this is the last time I hear it. Then he is out of the rinse water, and into a big soft towel. He dislikes the drying process even more than the bath, and he calls out again. When he is partially dry, Karen places him in front of the heating vent. In a few minutes, he looks like a pretty, feathery ball. Once completely dry, he licks himself all over, so that he smells like a cat again.

I am relieved and delighted to see him, but I hide my feelings and turn my back on him. Bad Cat! He has to know that he has upset me, and that I am angry with him. At least he should've shared his plans with me.

He comes to me slowly, rolls on his back exposing his vulnerability, to say he is sorry. I walk away and ignore him for a few hours to punish him. Then, I approach him. We rub each other and I lick him like a mama would lick a kitten. Later, we cuddle together on the big bed between Karen and Tony. We are a happy family again. I ask him about his adventures during his disappearance, but he is too tired to talk.

Our daily life continues as usual. Today, I am in the therapy room when Max visits Karen for the first time. He looks uncomfortable, and would prefer not to be there.

I am more precise about human ages now, but I have advanced very little in understanding human behaviour. Max is about seventeen, sloppy with untidy hair, and wears a crumpled shirt.

I hear him tell Karen, 'The doctor said I had to come to see you.' He gives Karen a letter.

'You don't have to be here, Max,' Karen says. You can leave any time, if you want to.'

'Well, now that I'm here, I suppose I'd better try to find some help.'

He looks at me for the first time. 'Hey Kitty Cat...nothing seems worthwhile lately does it?'

Karen listens for a long time, as he tells her how miserable he is.

I've said it before, Karen's patience and memory for what Humans say in this room is incredible. Unlike me, she doesn't become bored and fall asleep.

'I have tried talking to my parents, but they don't get it. They think starting a study course will help me, but it is not the answer. I don't have any answers...and sometimes I feel like giving up.'

He tells Karen that he is not sleeping well, eating very little and unable to concentrate on his studies.

Max is sick...another sad teenager. He is like a kitten who has lost his Catness. I hope that he comes to see Karen again before he becomes sadder.

At the end of their time together, he thanks Karen for listening to him, and comes to my baskets to pat my head. 'Cheers Kitty Cat,' he says. 'Maybe I'll see you again.'

'I hope to see you soon, Max,' Karen says.

Tony has been out early and returns with a friend. Together they carry heavy rocks into our small garden. They secure the wire fence by placing the rocks around its base, blocking all the holes. Oliver will not be able to run away again.

He is recovering from his adventure by sleeping most of the day. Karen seems worried about his thinness and feeds him special enriched food. He moves from his basket only to eat or go to his litterbox. I wait patiently to discover where he has been. He holds on to his story like a precious chicken wing. At last, tonight, he decides to tell me his story.

'The pads under my feet itched. All I wanted was to run. In my dreams, a wild cat talked to me, urging me to break out of my easy life, and be free. After weeks of struggling to resist the need to run away, eventually it overcame me.

Once the hole I dug was big enough to escape, there were no decisions for me to make. I was drawn to the field near the house. I stumbled over rubble and raced through the tall grass, aware of the smells and sounds of the many creatures that lived there. The sky was above me and I was free, living my dream.

The cold discouraged older cats from leaving the ease of their owner's homes. This meant that a large group of younger, wild cats were able to claim most of the field as their territory. I was not one of them. There were too many rules to obey in the big group. I avoided their scent boundaries and hunting areas. They survived by scrummaging in garbage bins and hunting small animals. The big group was safe from owls and foxes that preyed on their kittens, but it wasn't for me.

Fortunately, I connected with some of the other runaways. Together we established our own community and had territory on the edge of the field. Food was scarce and we mainly hunted for mice. I made no challenge for leadership of the group, and refrained from fights, but my dominance was easily established. When I filled my body to its full power and height, the other cats were aware of my strength. They avoided any contest with me. We managed to live together without major problems, apart from times when the females were in season, disrupting the peace by calling for mates.

A group of Humans lived in the field. Runaways too, I guess. They set up places to live with bricks, stones and tents. They made fires at night to keep warm and cooked meat they bought. They often called us, but their dogs lying next to the fire kept us away. One Human in our territory preferred to be alone. He erected a tent and made his own fire. There were no dogs with him, and he was pleased to have many of us around his fire at night. He had his favourites who slept with him in his tent, but I wasn't one of them.

Dogs living in the houses near the field were our greatest threat. Though they had food at home and were not hungry, they came to the field for the fun of hunting cats, or tormenting us. They are energetic, powerful creatures, but not much of a match for a fast cat up a tree. We are stealthy hunters able to sneak up and pounce before a kill. I found dogs stupid when not in packs or without a leader. In modern times, they are too accustomed to the easy life to be true hunters. Their barking and heaviness on their feet gave them away to a smart cat keen to survive.'

I do not agree with everything Oliver says about dogs. I have learned that they can be a formidable enemy.

'So what made you decide to come home?' I ask.

'The cold, discomfort and missing my home, you, Tony and Karen. My adventure was over. It was time to grow up, but I don't want to be like you – so settled and stable.'

Karen eats lunch and I have some of my pebbles. We sit quietly on the couch together. Our calm is interrupted by the ringing phone.

As Karen listens, her happy face disappears. 'Oh, I am so sorry that Tamara has passed...what a lovely young person...such a sad loss, but at least she is free from pain and at peace now.'

Sad Cat! Tamara had a deep kindness. I hope her spirit is free and resting now.

Karen stands and stretches like a cat.

'I'd like to rest for a while longer, but we have to leave soon, Bella. Benjamin is still in hospital and he has asked to see you.'

With my harness on and my lead in Karen's handbag, we leave for the hospital.

Today, we have no trouble finding the cancer ward and no one stops us to ask questions. Benjamin is sitting up in bed waiting for us.

'Hi, Princess...and Karen too. Thanks for paying a miserable dude a visit.'

'Good to see you, Benjamin.'

'Call me Benjy...please.'

I jump onto his bed, curl my tail around his arm and snuggle into his chest.

He has so much vitality that I hope with help from the doctors, he will fight back and recover.

'The doctor has just left. The news is that I need stronger chemo and radiation therapy for the tumour in my lung, but he was fairly positive and thinks it will help. I need Bella's soothing purrs to make me brave.'

As they talk, I close my eyes. I open them again when Benjy tells Karen that he was a massage therapist before he became ill. While in hospital, he has been studying to obtain further qualifications.

'I've massaged adults, children, horses and even dogs, but I've never worked on a cat. You're going to be the first cat, Princess...a present from me.'

He adjusts his pillows and pushes himself up to a sitting position.

'Right Princess, I'm putting you on your side. Say *meow*, if I'm hurting you, or if you want me to stop.'

His strong fingers travel down my spine from my head to my tail, finding the tight spots in my neck and back. He works on my legs and sore muscles that I don't know are there, and eases them. There are brief moments of discomfort followed by the pleasure of released tension.

What an incredible experience!

'That's it. You can sleep a little now,' he says. 'Your body will feel light and relaxed.'

I dream I am with my friend the duck. I have a cat's body with wings that allow me to fly. I am flying over my garden and all the houses I see from the half-tree.

Then I hear Karen's voice bringing me back to the hospital ward.

'Wake up, Bella,' we have to go.'

'If you're in the hospital, please visit me again Princess and Karen,' he says with a wave.

'Keep positive Benjy,' Karen says.

A nurse from the children's cancer ward asks us to visit some of the children to cheer them up.

'We are going there now,' Karen says.

It is a short walk from Benjy's bed to the children's ward. I can hear their young voices in the distance. The ward smells of strong antiseptics and sickness.

A nurse rushes towards us. 'You've brought Bella, great! There's going to be huge excitement in the ward.'

Karen takes me out of my carry box and attaches my lead.

'I think you're going to enjoy this, Treasure,' she says.

'She's here, the beautiful ginger cat!' One child calls out as she spots me. Then the others shout and their voices blend. 'Come to me!', 'I'm first', 'Me please!'

The nurse claps her hands. 'One at a time! Bella will come to each of you for five minutes.'

Karen takes me from bed to bed. Every child pats me or has a cuddle, and I purr for each one.

The sick children are all beautiful, and I can feel their loving, gentleness. I hope I am making them happy. Two of the children whisper to me and touch me kindly. I sense that these children love cats even more than the others. I beg Karen with my eyes, to stay with all of them a little longer.

She reads my message and we stay longer.

Oliver has put on weight and recovered, but I'm not sure if he has settled down. Even in the cool weather, he is outside almost every day. Now he is at our garden fence calling to other cats passing, some of them females. Though he is maturing emotionally, his body seems to be on another course. At night, he listens out for the wails of female cats in season, and his restlessness tells me that he wants to be with them. I think of the magnificent kittens Oliver could father. Trouble is definitely brewing.

Tony is discussing Oliver with Karen. 'He is developing quickly, but that is common with Siamese cats,' Tony says. 'We will have to watch him carefully. He is restless at night.'

'Perhaps he should be neutered now,' Karen remarks.

'Give him a little more time. He's still so young,' Tony says.

We are all in the television room after a quick meal Tony brings home.

'It's Chinese take out,' he says.

'A bit of chicken for each of you,' Karen says, placing a few bits on a plate. They enjoy the food and eat it with strange, thin sticks, but we don't like the smell or taste of the food and leave it on the plate.

'You cats don't know what you are missing. The trouble is that neither of you will try something new,' Tony says.

'Cat's like what they know is safe to eat, and has the taste they like,' Karen says with a shrug.

Once the food is cleared away, I curl up in Karen's lap and Oliver goes to Tony.

I am warm and cosy. It is time for Cat Contemplation:

I'm starting to change my mind about Tony. He has to be a decent, caring person, or Karen wouldn't love him as much as she does. He helps Karen a lot. He does vacuuming with the buzz machine. Often he brings home dinner so that she doesn't have to cook, and occasionally he washes up after the meal.

Oliver tells me how kind Tony is – that he gives him special tasty treats, makes toys for him and plays with him often. I must've come at the wrong time after Samantha, or perhaps Tony doesn't like ginger cats. I am glad that he is a happier Human now. Perhaps his job worries have been resolved. One day I hope he will like me more.

Huge Stinky Rats! I can smell it from a distance. Oliver has sprayed his pee on the carpet in the sitting room. This is the first time he has sprayed.

He is growing up and trying mark the house as his territory. I wish he had more self-control.

Karen cleans the carpet carefully with soap and disinfectant, and puts loads of pepper on the spot to stop him going there again.

'Not under any circumstances am I having Oliver spraying all over the house. Once is enough!' She says to Tony.

Oliver is asleep, as I listen to Karen and Tony discussing him. They agree that he has to be neutered.

'He is already looking out for females in season. It will get worse as he grows older, and we won't sleep much,' Tony says.

'I'm taking him to the vet tomorrow,' Karen adds. 'No more spraying or prowling. We are having him neutered, and that's final.'

The word vet makes my whiskers shiver, and neutered is the most awful word of all.

Early this morning, Karen wakes Oliver and puts him into his carry box. I hear him meowing all the way to the garage. Just as well he doesn't know his fate. The handsome Bengal at the cattery was neutered, and not at all happy about it.

I shudder as I remember Karen taking me to the vet to be neutered, or spayed, as Humans call it. It was a nasty operation to prevent me having kittens.

There I was in a sunspot for my first long snooze of the morning, when Karen woke me. Before I had time to protest, she grabbed me and put me inside my carry box. At the vet, two large dogs growled at me in the waiting area, but their owners had them on a tight lead.

'How long will Bella have to stay?' Karen asked a young nurse.

'Until tomorrow if all goes well.'

'I have something I'd like Bella to have... a shirt of mine. She'll be able to smell me with her, and not be as afraid,' Karen said.

Karen patted my head, whispered that she loved me, and would see me soon. I had no idea why I was there or what was going to happen to me. It was the first time she had left me in a strange place and I was scared. The nurse put me into a cage smelling of other animals. I cried as I rubbed the cage frantically to remove the odours. Then I sat on Karen's shirt and waited. I had no idea what I was waiting for.

The same tall vet with large hands, that had touched me before, felt me all over. He said that I was in good shape for the operation. Then he looked serious, and called one of the nurses to prepare me for surgery. I did not understand then what surgery was. Nor did I know what I was about to lose, and how I would feel about it later. All I felt was a tiny prick.

I woke up in my cage. I could smell Karen's scent and wished she was with me. I hurt and cried softly. The vet examined me, and then gave me an injection for pain. I floated off to somewhere in the future where all cats are loved. I was asleep for ages. When I woke, it was morning. Other cats around me told me what I had lost. They were there for the same operation.

I heard the vet say. 'She's fine and can go home now'.

Karen came to collect me. Once home, I slept a lot and ate little. Soon I was well, but furious.

What about *Cat Rights*, I thought. It was unfair and unjust! Karen had made the decision to have me spayed, and as a cat, I had no say in the matter.

However, now, after a long and hard think about it from all Cat Angles, I realise that having kittens may not have been the best idea. The life of feral kittens is uncertain. An uncared for Mama cat alone with kittens is even worse.

After six to eight weeks, if they survived, my kittens could've been taken from me. Perhaps the lucky ones may have found a good home, but others could've ended up with uncaring Humans, or even become wild and lived out of garbage tins, as so many cats do. Enough deep thinking about a painful subject, I tell myself.

I am restless as I await Oliver's return. When Karen brings him home, he refuses to eat and wants to sleep in his basket.

I am concerned about him, and hope he will be well in the morning. I hope too that he will stop spraying. During the night, I watch over him and lie next to him. It is strange that I feel so motherly towards him.

I did not realise that he had grown up, though all the signs were there. Perhaps he sprayed to send me a message, to tell me that he is a mature cat now – that the time has come for him to mark his area of the house. The house was mine before he came, but now I have decided to give him what he wants, or we will fight. There is enough space in the house for both of us – two scratch poles, three low windows, several places to run and to sleep at night. Some areas we can claim as our own, others we can share. He will mark his part of the territory as soon as he recovers.

I wonder if he understands the type of surgery he has undergone. I guess he will find out.

Another icy morning. As I wait for Oliver to wake, I sit at the vent to warm myself and think deeply.

Today is the day that he will claim his equal share of the house. Naturally, I want to keep my favourite spots, the ones where I spend most of my time. He can have his half of the rest. We will share the television room, and the big bed, as he sleeps on Tony's side and I am with Karen.

Once Oliver has eaten his breakfast, I tell him about my decision and wait for him to join me. Initially, he eyes me, unsure of my motives. Gradually he follows me, and begins to cover my scent on his portion of the house. I can tell he is thrilled to have his own, and equal, territory. When he has completed spreading his scent, he comes to me. We touch and rub. He gives me a nose kiss and his purr is deep and throaty.

Now we are equal and true friends. He is happy and I am too.

Max comes to see Karen again. He says he has been stressed, is not sleeping well and is hardly eating. He looks pale and dishevelled.

'Hey kitty cat…life can be tough,' he says. After he sits, he puts his head in his hands. 'The hassles with my parents, and school exams have stressed me out.'

They discuss Max's problems and I am about to nod off, when Karen suggests he tries meditation.

'An excellent idea – better than tablets. I tried it on my own once, but the trouble was that I started off okay, and then I couldn't hold my concentration. It's worth another try, I guess. If you do it with me, Karen, it might work,' he says with a shrug.

Every time Karen works with meditation, I listen and do it too. It is like a Cat Dream and I enjoy it.

Once Max settles in his chair, she talks to him in a soft, calm voice. I watch him take deep breaths, his eyes flutter and close. Then my eyes close too.

'Imagine that it is late afternoon and you're in a rambling garden filled with exquisite plants. You're sitting under a shady tree and watching the butterflies,' she says in her soothing voice.

I am in my garden. I am warm, the grass is soft and I am

under the half-tree. I watch the butterflies and try to catch them, but they fly away. As I listen to Karen's voice, they disappear.

When I wake Max has gone and Karen is working on her computer again.

Karen's phone rings, and I try to hear her side of the conversation.

'Oh yes, I remember, you were here for the cricket match. I hope you enjoyed it.'

'Goodness...is that what they said after you had the tests...definitely cancer in your leg...but at an early stage and they managed to cut it out. Bella knew, and she was trying to alert you to it...she is amazing! Well, thank you for letting me know. I hope that you recover soon,' she says.

Karen comes to my basket and strokes my head. 'You are an incredible cat and I love you lots and lots,' she says.

I am in Karen's therapy room when Jeremy and his mother arrive. Jeremy looks well and cheerful.

He runs to me and gives me a cuddle.

'Bella, Bella, I've brought you a present,' he says, as he pulls a toy mouse that moves from his pocket.

Meow, meow, I say, and rub my head against him in thanks.

Jeremy has gone to all the trouble of bringing me a present. How kind! He has a lot of caring Humanness in his small body.

The toy mouse is a poor imitation and moves slowly, but it doesn't matter. It smells of catnip, so it could provide some fun. He makes the toy mouse run for me, and while I pretend to chase it, I listen to his mother's comments.

'Jeremy has moved on and is happier and more independent. He is sleeping and eating well now too. His brother, Laurie, has kept his promise and popped in to see him. Last week he took Jeremy for an ice cream. It's his relationship with his father, that I'm a bit concerned about.'

Karen nods, as she often does. There are times when it seems to me that when Humans nod, it is often better than them talking.

Thank Cats! Jeremy is tired of the mouse game. I snuggle up to him while he talks to me, but continue to focus my attention on the conversation between Karen and his mother.

'Jeremy has been spending a lot more time with his dad over weekends. They went to the beach, had fish and chip dinners and saw fun movies together.' She shifts her position on the chair before continuing. 'That's all fine, but Jeremy tells me that his dad has a special girlfriend now. Jeremy doesn't say much about her, but a serious girlfriend is a lot for him to handle so soon after our break up. I guess I'm afraid that he won't have as much attention from his father now.'

Jeremy starts playing with the mouse again, but I don't show as much interest in it this time.

I am glad when Karen interrupts the game by asking, 'How are you enjoying being with your dad, Jeremy?'

Jeremy grins. 'It's great! Mum lets me stay up a bit later some nights so I can see him during the week. We are having fun on weekends. Laurie comes to visit me too. Next week Laurie and Dad are taking me fishing.'

'That's exciting!' Karen says. 'Is your Dad's new girlfriend coming fishing too?'

Jeremy shrugs. 'I don't know.'

'What is she like?'

He shrugs again. 'Okay!'

Karen and Jeremy's mother have an incredibly boring conversation about the girlfriend.

Cats Alive! What is his mother worrying about? They split up, so surely she isn't jealous. Just as well I'm a cat. Humans make their lives incredibly complicated.

Their conversation seems endless. I stop listening and fall asleep.

Thank Cats! Oliver has not sprayed again, and he has stopped wanting to run out at night. He is active and playful, retrieves balls thrown for him, and likes playing games like Hide and Seek. When Tony is at work and Karen is busy, we play together, wrestling, or chasing each other, and he wins every time. We give each other quick nips, but we don't fight. He is not aggressive towards me, and he has become more affectionate to both Tony and Karen. I like him a lot more now.

Cat Sleep! I am happy and make the best of the cooler months by sleeping in my basket or near the heating vents. I enjoy sleeping so much. It is of key importance to cats. Like me, Oliver finds heated spots for sleep near the vents. We are both independent cats, but we keep warm during cold nights by cuddling up together. During the heat of summer, we will sleep alone.

Being comfortable, feeling wanted and having a full stomach is the secret to good cat sleep.

Karen is extremely busy! More Humans seem to feel sad, worried and lost during the cold weather. Her phone rings all the time with requests for appointments. She can't refuse to see sad Humans. Instead, she makes extra time for them by having a shorter lunch, or starting work earlier and finishing later. Of course, I worry that she will exhaust herself.

When she is busy, I am busy too, doing my work comforting troubled children and teenagers. I try hard to help as many of them as I can.

I enjoy being busy and helpful.

Life in Catland is pleasant and I have no complaints. The food is excellent. Karen knows the brand of food we enjoy most, and she provides us with treats most nights. The atmosphere in the television room at night is peaceful. Oliver sits on Tony's lap, while I remain close to Karen. I am happy that our owners are sitting together, laughing, touching often, and kissing.

I made a huge error. Life was wonderful in Catland until this morning.

I woke to find our house dark and icy. We are experiencing an electricity outage today. I am frozen, and I can hardly feel the tips of my ears. Humans seem to manage the cold more effectively than we do, by wearing many layers of clothing to insulate them from the cold. We have only one thick, warm coat for winter.

Last night, I had one of my dreams about water – a bad omen, so I shouldn't be surprised to find something unpleasant happening.

I was running through tall undulating grassland when clouds banked up, the sky darkened, and down poured heavy rain. To escape the loathsome rain, I ran and ran until I found dry shelter under some rocks. I stayed there, tired, cold, hungry and scared, but the rain didn't stop.

Karen is keeping warm by wearing a coat and gloves inside the house. She is asking all the people due to see her today to bring a blanket with them. Just as well she remembers to fill our bowls with extra food for energy.

Tonight, the cold house without electricity is extremely unpleasant. Karen and Tony are so cold that they are wrapped in blankets. They also complain that there is no television. To find their way in the house, they hold light beams, they call torches, and place candles in all the rooms. Karen is aware how cold we are and lines our baskets with fluffy blankets. Just as well Oliver and I sleep bathed in each other's body heat.

The outage continues for another day. Tony arrives home with a box of logs that carry the scents of many creatures and plants. We sniff them and wonder where they come from. He takes a few logs to the sitting room and after several attempts at lighting them, he manages to start a fire. A slow, wisp of a flame grows, turns shades of blue and orange, and magically the room is warm. Tony and Karen settle in front of the fire and we sit with them.

Without television as a distraction, Tony and Karen talk. He shares his memories of his youth with Karen, of nights spent with his parents and grandfather, Pops, around a fire in their farmhouse. He sighs, and his expression changes to sadness.

'I wish I had met your parents, but they were gone before we met,' Karen says, as she puts her arm around him.

Tony replies, 'The night of the fire, I was at boarding school and Mum and Dad were alone in the house. Pops wasn't there then. He was away on his first holiday in many years. Dad lit a fire, but they were both tired after work, and fell asleep. By the time they realised the house was burning, it was too late. I can't help thinking, even now, that if I had been at home instead of at boarding school, they might have survived the fire.'

'It must've been a dreadful time for you. I know it still upsets you,' Karen says and gives him a hug.

'This is the first fire I've lit since the farmhouse caught alight that night.' He sighed. 'Mum and Dad should've sold the farm, when Pops advised them to sell it. The endless hard work was overwhelming. When my uncle wanted to buy it from them, they refused to sell. They had lived there all their married life and it was part of them. Pops realised that they were worn out with the battle of running the farm, and by then he was too old to help them. If only they had taken his advice.'

'It's a magnificent piece of land, and an exquisite view of the mountains! You can't blame them for wanting to stay on, but they needed a lot more help. Fires are monsters. I'm so sorry, my darling. I know you miss them terribly, but just as well you are close to your grandfather. He has been like a father to you. I love him too.'

What a tragedy! Poor Tony! His story makes me think of little Dane who witnessed the fire next door, and how badly it affected him. I feel sorry for Tony for the first time.

Oliver is upset for Tony too. He knows about fire. When he ran away, a house near the field was on fire. The Humans inside were screaming and the huge, plumes of smoke were frightening.

He goes to Tony, sits, on his lap and nuzzles close to him.

'Oliver, my boy, you understand,' Tony says in a voice choked with emotion.

'Oliver can hear the sadness in your voice...and Siamese are very sensitive. He's grown into a loving cat.' Karen comments.

Tony and Karen are eating their breakfast when the phone rings. It is a friend of Tony's grandfather, who tells them that Pops is in hospital. During the electricity outage, Pops became disoriented in the dark, slipped and fell. He lay alone and in pain, unable to move until his friend found him this morning and called an ambulance.

Tony looks upset and rushes to the hospital. He returns later, and tells Karen that his grandfather is recovering and should be out of hospital the following day. He sits with his head in his hands, thinking what to do for his grandfather when he leaves hospital. Karen puts her arms around him.

'I love Pops and I'm so sorry he fell. He won't be able to care for himself. It will be no trouble at all looking after him here until he feels stronger. I'll make up a bed for him and you'll be able to spend time with him when you come home from work. I know you would like that,' she says with a smile.

Tony gives her a hug and kiss. 'I'd like to help him. He cared for me whenever I needed him.'

Karen tidies the back room and all is ready for Pops to stay.

'I hope the electricity will be back on by the time he comes...but we'll cope if it isn't,' she says.

Tony helps Pops up the steps to the house. The old man's face is white with pain, and he battles not to groan too loudly or cry out.

Karen welcomes him and helps Tony to make his grandfather comfortable. The house is still cold, but Karen manages to make hot food for Pops on a small stove with blue gas flames that smells disgusting.

'If I'm not wrong he's an animal lover,' Karen says.

'I know he likes dogs, but I don't think he's keen on cats,' Tony replies.

Oh well, our lives will be turned upside down with him coming to stay if he prefers dogs. I guess he will be in the bed in the back room where Oliver stayed after I rescued him. It's not worth worrying about.

Cats in Heaven! The house is warm again tonight, and the lights are back on. The vents radiate heat. I'm so happy! Pops lies in a warm bed, and both Karen and Tony are caring for him. Oliver and I keep away from the old man who dislikes cats.

I continue to work in the therapy room with Karen. She is busy, and caring for Pops takes almost all her remaining time. Oliver complains that Tony's attention is on his grandfather now, instead of him.

Curiosity takes me to the back of the house. Cautiously, I peek round the open door. The frail, old man is in bed. At first, he is unaware of me. Then uncertainly, he gropes for his glasses.

'I see someone at the door,' he says, in a kind voice.

I wonder about this old man, who Tony believes dislikes cats. Taking a risk, I step hesitantly into the room. I can run away if he shouts at me.

'Come and say hello to me,' he murmurs. 'I have a dog, and my friend is looking after him while I'm here. I haven't owned a cat since I was a child. His name was Cocoa and I adored him.'

He manages to push himself up on the pillows. His shaking hand pats the cover on his bed for me to join him. I jump onto the bed.

'Oh, you are a beauty, and with such knowing eyes. We are going to have a lovely time together while I'm here.'

His wrinkled face is kind. He is Tony's grandfather, but a sensitive, empathic man, and nothing like his grandson. I feel a connection with this old man and want to be near him. My paw touches his hand and he smiles.

'You are a special cat, aren't you?'

He strokes my head and whispers kind words to me. After our brief encounter, I know that I will love him.

His unsteady hand adjusts his glasses. 'Will you let me look at your name tag on your collar?' He asks.

I bend forward for him.

'So, you're Bella. A perfect name for a beautiful ginger cat,' he says.

'It's a strange thing Bella, but I have this feeling...and I'm old enough to trust my feelings. It is a feeling that you understand what I am saying, and the way I feel. Stranger still, I can sense what you feel – that you like and trust me. The same thing happened with my cat Cocoa, bless him. He crossed the rainbow bridge so many years ago.' The old man makes himself more comfortable. 'I think we were meant to meet, Bella. I don't believe in coincidences.'

How can Tony have a grandfather with such a deep connection to cats, and with me in particular, while Tony tolerates me for Karen's sake? I wonder if Pops will connect with Oliver?

The old man talks and I listen. He tells me how he fell in the dark during the power outage. He was severely bruised and sore, but fortunate not to have broken any bones.

He goes on to talk about his mother, father, and sisters, and how they all lived on the family farm together, when he and Cocoa were young. There were sheep, four dogs, seven horses and six cats, but Cocoa was his own cat. He smiles as he relates that the other animals were scared of Cocoa, who could be vicious if threatened. Cocoa had the run of the farm, and he delighted in jumping on the woollen backs of the sheep. In winter, Cocoa and the other cats slept with the sheep to keep warm. He laughs loudly, as he describes how his cat behaved like a dog, herding stray lambs back to their mothers.

Suddenly he is quiet, and tears fill his eyes. He wipes them away quickly. 'The worst thing that happened in my life was the terrible fire on the farm.' More tears flow. 'My son and daughter-in-law were burned alive on their farm while I was away enjoying myself – my first holiday in years. It was irresponsible of me. I should've realised the strain the farm was causing my children.' He sighs deeply. 'At least Tony was at school at the time, and saved from the fire.' He tries to control his tears but in vain. 'He's like a son to me and I love him deeply, and Karen too, but I carry enormous guilt, and I grieve the senseless loss of my children.'

I nestle closer, understanding his pain and sadness.

'You understand Bella...I know that,' He says, as he pats my head.

When Tony comes home after work, he sees me on his grandfather's bed and is astounded. 'I didn't know that you liked cats, Pops.'

The old man smiles. 'You don't know everything about me Tony. Bella is staying with me, unless Karen needs her,' his grandfather says emphatically.

'Of course, if you want her here,' Tony says, sounding surprised.

I am busy and don't have as much sleep as usual between my job in the therapy room and being with Pops, but I enjoy being needed. Oliver watches me and learns. He is a smart and highly sensitive cat. I sense that he wants to follow in my paw steps.

After my work with Karen, I find Oliver on the old man's bed.

'This little beauty has a kind nature,' Pops says.

I join Oliver on the bed, and the old man smiles happily.

'Now I have both of you with me. How lucky can an old man be?'

Later, when Pops leaves his bed to hobble around the house, Little Blue Eyes follows him. I am happy to watch how gentle he is with the old man. I leave them together. When Pops returns to bed, Oliver curls up next to him.

'I'm feeling much stronger, so I'm going home tomorrow,' he says to me.

Cat Alert! I give him a long look.

'Yes, Bella, I know you think I should stay here for a few more days, but I miss my home. I promise to visit you, special one, and sweet Oliver too.' He stops to gather his strength before continuing. 'Please look after Karen and Tony. I hope that they will have a child soon. It's selfish of me, but I long for a grandchild before I die.'

After a session of energetic chasing each other and wrestling, Oliver says he wants to ask me something important. 'How can I learn to be a Therapy Cat like you?'

'You can't learn to be one. You have to like Humans, and be tolerant of their strangeness – and you have to want to help them, especially the young ones. They are different to us in so many ways. A Therapy Cat may even need to help other animals who are sick – horses for example.'

'But, do you think I could be any good at it one day?' He asks. 'I would like to be able to help the way you do. It is a special job, and important.'

'It's about having an easy-going temperament, generosity

and empathy, Oliver. Either you have it, or you don't. You can't learn it. If you have the temperament, you can learn some added ways of helping.

He seems unsatisfied by my answer and moves towards the warmest heat vent.

I was being kind. Oliver is clever, and he is turning into a good friend. He's also becoming more handsome every day. I look at his silky coat, slender graceful body and his finely chiselled features, and realise once again that he is nothing like me. I think of his long slender tail that swishes when he is bored – and, that he is often bored. He is sensitive to his own needs, and to Tony's needs, but I wonder if he is tolerant and caring enough to help all sad and sick Humans. I'm not sure if he has the qualities of a Therapy Cat?

Mia is here to see Karen with her mother. She hasn't visited me for a while, and I notice a change in her. She is even taller since I saw her last. Her step is confident and her eyes are smiling.

'Karen, we came today to tell you that I am well now. We wanted to thank you for all your help. I'm not afraid of the school bullies now.'

'Mia couldn't have done it without your help, Karen,' her mother says.

'And thank you, too, darling Bella.' Mia says, nodding in my direction.

'I think Mitzi, the cat belonging to the man next door has helped Mia too. She can't have her own cat due to her dad's allergy, but he allows her to play with Mitzi whenever she likes.'

'I am pleased to see you looking so well, Mia, and that you have Mitzi to play with now,' Karen says.

Mia tells Karen that her teacher is a piano player, and that a week ago, her teacher accompanied her on the piano, while she played popular tunes for her classmates on the violin. The children knew the songs, and joined in clapping and singing. It was a huge success and everyone had fun.

I can tell by Karen's smile how pleased she is with Mia's recovery.

Mia talks on happily about her new school friends.

Then she asks, 'Where is Oliver, your beautiful Siamese kitten? I saw him last time I was here.'

Karen leaves and returns quickly carrying Oliver.

'He's absolutely adorable. Come to me, Oliver,' Mia calls, but Oliver does not go to her. He hides behind the chair. When she calls him again, he pokes his head out, but refuses to approach her. He is unhappy about going to this strange child.

Now I am certain he will not be a Therapy Cat, even if he would like to be one. He slips out of the room, and I hear him running towards the heat vent.

'Oliver is shy. Don't be upset that he won't come to you,' Karen says soothingly.

I go to Mia for a hug, while Mia's mother talks to Karen for a while longer.

Mia wipes away a few tears when she cuddles me for the last time.

'I will miss you lots, Bella,' she whispers.

I will miss her too.

Oliver refuses to talk about the way he acted with Mia. He is ashamed, and pretends it didn't happen.

One morning he says, 'I guess I'm not suited to being a Therapy Cat. I am not comfortable with Humans I haven't met before.'

'Being a Therapy Cat is not for every cat, Oliver. Don't let it bother you,' I say.

But he is bothered, and a little jealous. He is not walking as proudly as usual. He wants to feel special too.

Pops visits late this afternoon. He says he is well now, but he misses Karen and Tony. He gives me a sidelong glance to tell me that he misses me too.

Karen invites him to stay for dinner. Instead going to the television room before dinner to talk to Tony, he finds me.

'Bella, I've been lonely this week. I thought of you, and wished you could've been with me.'

He sits in a comfortable chair and I jump onto his lap. He strokes me and I nestle close and purr.

'I wish you lived with me, Bella. You understand, even more than my dog, Rusty. I pretend to be tough, but since my fall, I'm afraid that I will be unable to care for myself – that I'll be a burden to Tony and Karen. I'm doing my best to keep fit, eat well and exercise. It's all I can do.'

I keep purring, and place my paws around his neck to tell him that I care about him.

Later, while Karen, Tony and Pops have dinner, I hear them talking about Oliver.

Pops says, 'Oliver is an incredibly handsome cat. There's a cat show in this area in three weeks. I think Oliver has a good chance of winning. It's worthwhile, the top three cats win prizes of free food for a year and there are rosettes too.'

Tony laughs. 'Why not, if you do all the preparation for the show.'

Could Oliver win a ribbon and a prize? It will be interesting.

'If you want to enter him into the show, Pops, you had better start working on him soon. There's a huge amount of preparation – shampooing, combing his fur and the rest,' Karen reminds him. 'I put Samantha on show once and she won a special mention, but what a lot of work!'

The next day, Pops arrives with a basket filled with cat shampoo, conditioner, towels, combs, brushes, and nail clippers. He borrows Karen's hair dryer and is ready to start Oliver's beauty treatment. Oliver knows nothing about the old man's intentions, as he sniffs the bottles and combs. When he hears the water running in the laundry trough, he remembers the bath Karen gave him after he had run away, and tries to hide. Pops finds him and the beautifying of Oliver begins.

Top of Pops' list is claw clipping. It is Oliver's first experience of having his claws clipped. He is a young cat with fine, long, sharp claws that badly need a trim. Oliver squirms complaining loudly, but in vain. Pops holds him firmly, as he clips the tips of Oliver's claws. Oliver is indignant. Next, Pops brushes Oliver's coat vigorously and then combs away all the dead hairs. Oliver enjoys that part.

He has forgotten the water in the laundry tub, and just as well. Pops adds a bubbling cat shampoo to the warm water. Then he puts Oliver into the trough and there are loud meows. The final rinse and conditioner to make his fur glossy is too much for Oliver. His resistance reaches high notes. Out he comes, wet, bedraggled, and shivering. Pops part dries him in a soft towel, and then with Karen's hair dryer. Once dry, his fur is soft and glistening, but he is miserable. For enduring the lengthy beauty ritual, Pops treats Oliver to tuna with shrimp. He gives me some too.

I wonder if there will be another shampoo and brush ordeal before the competition.

Karen and Tony are thrilled when they see Oliver looking stunning. Karen picks him up and cuddles him.

Tony kisses Oliver's head. 'I'm sure you will win a prize. After all, who could resist you?'

Bored Cats! I turn away from all the fuss about Oliver, and enjoy the warmth of the heating instead.

A mother and her five-year-old, only child, Sophie, enter the therapy room. Sophie is friendly with dark hair and eyes as blue as Oliver's. The mother talks a lot, and fast. She is concerned that Sophie has an imaginary friend.

'Sophie expects me to make meals for her pretend friend, help her to dress and wash her hair in the shower,' she explains. 'When Sophie is naughty, she blames her little pretend friend for it. Surely at five, she should be growing up and finding real friends. It doesn't seem right.'

What in Catland is an imaginary friend? Well, I guess I play with a pretend friend too. Before Oliver arrived I was lonely and played with a white pretend cat who visited me every day. She's gone now that I play with Oliver.

'My special friend's name is Charlotte...Lottie. Mum doesn't like her, but she's my friend. I like her, and I'm not letting her go. I asked Lottie if I can talk to you, Karen, and to the kitty about her, and she says it's okay.'

'I would like to know about Lottie. I'm sure Bella would like to know about her too,' Karen says.

'Lottie is pretty and a little older than me. She knows lots of things, and helps me to feel better if I'm scared at night. We play games together with fairies, we paint and dance. It's fun!'

Karen turns to Sophie. 'Lottie sounds special and a very important friend to you, but is she real?'

Sophie laughs. 'She's my best friend, but of course she's not real. She lives in my head.'

'Will she ever grow out of having this little friend?' Sophie's mother asks.

'Don't be concerned,' Karen tells Sophie's mother. 'Many young children have imaginary friends that help them with real things that scare or worry them. Their pretend friends usually stay a while, until they are no longer needed. As Sophie grows older, you can help her by involving her in enjoyable real experiences with other children, and by being there for her. When she builds up confidence and has other friends, her pretend friend will leave.'

'Maybe it would help if I asked some of the mothers to visit with their children. It would be an opportunity to play together,' Sophie's mother says.

'An excellent idea...and perhaps consider a pet for Sophie as well. Dogs and cats are real friends too.'

'I wish I could have a kitten,' Sophie says.

'Okay Sophie, I'll talk to your dad about a kitten for you.'

'If you are still worried about Sophie come and see me again,' Karen says.

Sophie and her mother are both smiling when they leave.

After seeing Sophie and her mother, Karen puts her head on her desk and rests for a few minutes.

'That's it for the day, my treasure,' she says.

I sit on Karen's lap, and as we relax, I feel loved inside. I am about to fall asleep, when I sniff her. She smells slightly different today, neither sour nor sweet. I move closer to sniff her again. What is causing her to smell strange? I cannot recall her ever smelling like this before.

Cat Alert! The following day when I sit on her lap, I am aware once more of the unusual smell of her body. I place my head on her tummy, and sense almost undetectable vibrations. I am certain now. She has a tiny, human kitten growing inside her, but perhaps she is not aware of it yet. I place my paws on the new life inside her and lick her tummy. Then I look at her, and purr.

'What are you up to Bella?' She says with a laugh. 'You are acting very strangely today. What are you trying to tell me?'

I purr loudly for her.

The day of the cat show arrives. Oliver is subjected to another wash and dry, as well as a last comb with a touch of jell rubbed into his coat. His tail is flicking at a fast rate to register his utter displeasure.

Pops smiles broadly. 'You look like a Prince of a Cat, Oliver. Be confident, I'm sure you'll win an award.'

Proud Cats! Oliver looks incredibly handsome. I'm thrilled for him and hope he wins. But, all this emphasis on superficiality is not my thing. It's the cat inside – Catness that counts most for me. However, I want him to be a Happy Cat, and he hasn't been as contented as usual lately. If this competition works for him, it will be a positive thing.

The day passes slowly for me, as I wonder if he has won any awards. At last, they return from the show. Pops is smiling broadly, and Oliver is ecstatic with a purr reaching high decibels. Proudly, Pops shows off Oliver's rosette. He won second prize for the best neutered cat on show.

'He was the most handsome by far. He should've won first prize, but the judges have their reasons, I guess,' the old man says.

Tony is thrilled. 'Second place is wonderful, and it calls for a celebratory drink all round.' He gives Oliver's tummy a rub. 'What a beauty you are!' He says lovingly.

He brings out a large bottle of clear, yellow liquid and glasses. We cats are given sliced beef treats from a packet.

Then Oliver sits on Tony's lap and is petted lavishly. Later, Tony takes Oliver's winning rosette and places it amongst the family photographs.

'It's a great win and his rosette should be in an important place,' he says to Karen.

She smiles and nods. 'I think we should donate the year's cat food Oliver won to Cat Rescue, so that other cats who have been rescued can benefit like Oliver and Bella have,'she says.

'That's a great idea...I agree,' Tony says giving her a hug.

I look at Oliver with loving half closed eyes and he returns my affection. He is pleased with Tony's suggestion.

After Tony pets Oliver again, he sits on the carpet and washes himself thoroughly. 'Smelling of human perfumes and gels is most undignified for a cat,' he says to me. 'I need to smell like me again.'

Karen calls me. 'You are my beauty, Bella,' she says. 'I don't need a cat show competition to tell me how beautiful and special you are.'

After the excitement, Oliver runs around the house a few times to burn off the energy he controlled during the day. He is pleased with himself. The win has lifted his mood, and he walks proudly again. His slender tail is straight and high expressing his joy. Though he says nothing about the judging experience, I guess that being prodded and examined by strange Humans was not fun. I give him head butts to congratulate him, but I don't want to spoil his pleasure with too many questions.

'We are both special,' I say to him. 'I am a Therapy Cat and you are a Show Cat. Isn't that wonderful.'

'Absolutely!' He says. 'We are lucky that Karen and Tony rescued us and care for us, but they are lucky to have us too. They have two very special cats.'

By now we are both purring.

Since his win at the cat show, Oliver has been naughty again. Yesterday, he tried to climb the curtains, but with his claws trimmed, he was unable to reach the top. Then, he pulled the cover off the big bed, and dragged it through the house to demonstrate his strength. Now that he has grown, he can jump up to low door handles, and prod them until they open. Opening cupboards are easy for him too.

Karen has told him to "settle down", and said "no" to him a few times, but he takes more notice of Tony. When Oliver showed off last night by opening a door after Tony closed it, he made Tony so angry that he sprayed Oliver with water.

He will stop showing off eventually, or spend time in the laundry as I did.

When we are in the garden, I usually keep one eye open, in case Oliver tries to hang on the branches of the half-tree. He may fall, or get up to some other mischief. His name ought to be "Mischief".

Today, watching him is tiring. I drift off to sleep and dream one of my favourite dreams in an earlier life.

I am in an enormous sacred place where Humans wearing long, white clothes that almost touch the ground, walk slowly, quietly and with dignity. There are many cats about, and each one is respected. We guard the sacred place for the Humans.

I am annoyed when my intriguing dream is interrupted by slurping sounds. I follow the noise to the wire fence.

Honey's pointed nose and tongue is poking through the fence. I am horrified. She is licking Oliver's face.

Jumping Rats! He is not only allowing her to lick him, but he is purring with delight.

What in Catland is happening with Oliver and Honey? I am both revolted and astounded!.

Meeowwwwww! I call to Karen, but she is talking on her hand phone again.

'Shush, shush!' She says to me.

Meeeow meeeow! I insist.

'Bella is going crazy...I'll call you back.'

She follows me outside. Then she laughs so much that she wipes her eyes.

'Really, Bella! Honey likes Oliver, and he is enjoying the attention. You dislike dogs and don't approve, that's all.'

She opens the fence gate and allows Honey into our garden. I stand back as the small dog bounds in. I prepare to climb the half-tree if necessary. With a yelp, Honey runs towards me, her tail wagging furiously. I stand my ground while she comes closer.

Wuff, wuff,

Oliver runs to her. I move forward cautiously.

'Let's play,' Oliver says, as he chases Honey.

Disgusted with Oliver, I stand back, as I watch them run after each other, roll, and pretend to fight. They play and have fun.

Cat Learning! It seems that I made a big mistake about Honey, one of my worst ever. She is more like a cat than I thought, and is nothing like the aggressive dogs I know. She has no intention of harming us, but that doesn't mean that I like her, or her smell.

I think of the dog who helped the blind man at the hospital, and all the therapy dogs who visit and help sick Humans in the same way as I do. I realise that my personal experience has biased me against dogs. There is a lot I have to learn about dogs. I have made a serious error of judgement, thinking all dogs were the same – nasty, wild, smelly, cat haters and dangerous. Some are like that, but I need to be a more Flexible Cat in my thinking about dogs...and everything in future.

Mid-Winter

The world is white outside, and soft, fluffy, wetness falls from the sky. It is not like rain, but cold and watery. I shudder. I tried walking in it only once, and rushed inside to dry myself next to a heating vent. Even in the heated house, Karen is wearing two jumpers, so it must be cold.

She rubs her hands together and says to Tony, 'The snow is pretty, but it is cold and slippery. Just as well it doesn't snow here often.'

Oliver looks at the pretty, white, outdoor world longingly. He is intrigued by its smoothness and the falling flakes from the sky.

His quivering nose and wide-eyed expression tells me that he is longing to go outside and experience the whiteness.

I say nothing to him. He is a mature cat now and he must make his own choices.

Meow, Meow, he says to Karen, as he stands at the cat door leading to our garden.

'Seriously Oliver, you want to go out into the snow?'

She laughs, as she opens the door. A rush of cold air follows as Oliver runs out. Quickly, she closes the cat door. The flakes are falling slowly, as he runs onto the whiteness. His footprints make indentations as he searches for the once familiar rocks and bushes all covered in white now.

I can't believe it. He is rolling in the snow, jumping and sliding. He tries to climb the half-tree but slips down. He tries again by jumping up to the wet branches and clinging to them. He uses his strength to reach the bottom branch of the tree. Then, cautiously, he climbs a little higher. He sits on the branch and looks out on the white world below.

'He's like a beautiful snow statue,' Karen says.

She calls Tony.

'Isn't he amazing…and how beautiful,' Tony says.

I am impressed at Oliver's strength and perseverance, and his desire to claim his territory, even in the wet snow. I certainly wouldn't go out there, or even attempt to climb the tree. Now that's brave Catness!

Oliver slides down the tree trunk, and runs to the cat door. Karen opens it and laughs as he shakes himself. He doesn't even look in my direction, but runs straight to the heating vent.

After this experience in the snow, he doesn't ask to go out again. We play indoors or sit near the vents to keep warm.

Tony is turning twenty – nine on the weekend and Karen is giving him a birthday party. He seems very old to me. I will be lucky to reach sixteen or possibly a little more, in human years. She has begun to bake sweet things and put them in the icy cold fridge. I hear her say that about seventy people are expected. Due to the cold, everyone will be inside. I am sure that both of us will be in the back room for most of the time.

Though I will hate it, feeling crushed amongst so many Humans could be far worse.

Today it is Tony's birthday. Karen is up early to make him a special breakfast of pancakes and to give him a present. He revels in the love and attention and likes his present – something to do with computers. She puts a blue bow around Oliver's neck and I have to endure a pink bow.

Rotten Rats! Bows on cats are ridiculous.

Liz and Pops are here to celebrate Tony's birthday, and two of Karen's friends are helping with moving the furniture from the sitting room to make more space for the guests. With all the noise and rushing, I find a safe warm spot and keep out of Liz's way.

I vehemently dislike things being changed or moved in our house. Routine and predictability is, as always, extremely important. I prefer everything to remain the same in our house, and I know that Oliver does too.

As I expected, Karen locks us in the back room before the guests arrive.

'Be good, you two,' she says.

Though we are at the back of the house, we can hear the guest's footsteps, their laughter and talking.

'Humans are very strange indeed,' Oliver says, his blue eyes puzzled.

'Agreed, and the longer you live with them, the stranger they will seem,' I say.

A loud banging noise is followed by Tony talking louder than usual. He thanks everyone for celebrating with him, for their good wishes and their gifts.

To gain everyone's attention, he bangs loudly again. 'We have some wonderful news to share with you all. Karen is expecting a baby in a few months and we are absolutely thrilled.'

The room erupts in clapping and calling out, "congratulations".

'I am happy that she knows now, and that she and Tony are sharing their good news,' I say to Oliver, purring loudly.

Oliver is bewildered. 'Karen is going to have a kitten ... and you knew?'

I purr again.

'Her body had an unusual smell. It took me some time to realise that it was similar to the smell of cats carrying kittens.'

'I missed it completely,' he says. 'But I'm not as close to Karen as you are.'

I don't tell Oliver that I have realised something important. He may laugh at me. Humans are animals – big ones with two legs – fur on their heads and only a little on their bodies. We are animals too, though we have fur coats and four legs. Though we are very different, in some way we are connected, and similar. That is how I managed to recognise the smell of a kitten baby on the way.

The noise lessens at last, and we hear Karen's footsteps.

'Time for you two to make an entrance,' she says. She carries Oliver out of the room first and returns for me.

'Our two lovely cats,' she says, introducing us to the guests.

The cat lovers amongst the group circle around us. We both enjoy the attention and the admiring words said about us.

Yummow! The best part is the food. Karen gives us a plate each of assorted delights.

Then, she returns us to the back room. Footsteps and talking outside the house finally tells us that the party is over. The guests are departing. Soon, there are sounds of the furniture being moved back into place, and the vacuum buzzing. Thankfully, Karen frees us, Liz has gone, and the house is ours again.

Today is a holiday, and we all sleep late. An atmosphere of relaxation fills the house. I sit next to Karen on the couch, wind my tail around her, and purr.

She looks at me. 'You are the most incredible, special cat Bella, and I love you so much. A few weeks ago, you licked my tummy and patted it with your paws. You were telling me that I was going to have a baby – a human kitten. I don't know how you knew, but you are correct. Tony and I are absolutely thrilled. Pops, Liz, and my dad and sister are happy for us too, but all our lives are going to change.'

I love Karen and I'm happy for her too, but *Oliver and I will have to learn to adapt to the changes or we will lose some of our Catness.*

I hardly recognise Emma when she walks into Karen's room. She has the same curvaceous shape, but other things have changed about her. It is difficult to put a "paw on it", but she seems brighter, and her voice is happier.

'Before I tell you my news, I want to thank you for taking Bella to visit my friend Ava in hospital. Ava is home now, and much stronger. Seeing and touching you, Bella, lifted her spirits.' She looks at me and smiles before continuing. 'Ava told me a strange story. When her food arrived with some chicken for Bella as well, Ava wasn't at all hungry. But, Bella wanted the chicken, and she nagged Ava to eat too. She put her paw firmly on Ava's arm, and stared hard at her. When Bella ate her food, Ava began to eat too...and that was the start of her recovery.'

I listened intently as Karen and Emma talked about a cat's ability to help and heal.

Too few people know that our purr and our loving cuddles can heal. I'm pleased that Ava is recovering.

'I'm sorry I haven't been to see you for ages, but I am doing my homework now...most of the time...and I think it is helping me,' Emma says.

'Well, you're looking great...and I hope you are feeling good too.'

'I have stopped being so obsessed about losing weight, and I like myself a little more.' She smiles shyly. 'I have some new friends and a boyfriend.'

While they talk, I doze, catching snatches of their conversation. I am alerted when Emma mentions the word "cat".

'It must be great to be a cat like Bella – loved, no self-image problems and always in the same coat.'

Karen laughs.

'Hey, Bella!' Emma says in a soft voice.

I am asleep after an early breakfast, when a loud noise wakes me.

'The truck and the men have arrived,' Tony shouts to Karen. 'They can start work inside first...if that's okay with you.'

Oliver is awake now, too. We are both at the window trying to see what is happening. Three huge Humans in dark overalls are unloading large boxes and equipment. Tony greets them and they follow him into the house through the back door.

'We'd better lock up the cats,' I hear him tell Karen. 'I have already moved their litterboxes, food and water.'

Rat's Poo! What in Catland is going on in our house this time?

Before we have time to consider what to do, Karen picks me up and Tony has Oliver in his arms.

Meow! meow! They ignore our calls of distress and carry us to the back room.

'Sorry cats. Both of you will have to stay in this room while the men are working inside the house. There's everything you need in here. It will be home for a while,' Karen says.

More Rat's Poo! Never a day without something interfering with our routine.

Oliver and I look at each other. 'What's going on,' he asks.

'I don't know. We'll have to wait and see,' I tell him.

Neither of us can sleep in our prison. As far as we are concerned, the banging and strange mechanical noises throughout the day are a major inconvenience. Karen comes into the room occasionally to give us more food or water, and then leaves again. Only when the weak sunlight departs for the day, does the noise stop.

We are confined to the back room in discomfort and misery for many days as the big human workers bang and knock. When at last, quiet is restored, Karen opens the door to allow us into the house, and to our horror and utter disgust, we find that part of the wall near the bedrooms no longer exists. Instead, heaps of dust and wires cover the floor.

I ask myself, why they are destroying our house? It was fine before. It must have something to do with the kitten baby in Karen's tummy. They want more space for it, but I can't see why. Our house is enormous already, and they want even more space! Anyway, why should we worry. The bigger the house the more territory we have.

'Cats, keep away from the mess. It's dangerous,' Tony warns.

Of course Oliver doesn't listen, he snoops amongst the rubble on the floor, and soon he is covered in fine dust.

As Tony brushes him, he says, 'A bath for you if I can't get rid of the dust.'

Oliver's eyes grow wide, but since playing in the snow, wetness is not as terrifying as it once was. Tony manages to clear the dust from his fur with a fine comb and a wet rub down. Oliver shivers, shakes himself, and then runs to the heat vent.

Karen asks Tony. 'Do you think the room will be big enough for the baby?'

So, I was correct. They are making a new room for the baby in Karen's tummy...when it comes out,' I tell Oliver.

Karen is not working while the knocking and banging is happening, but I wouldn't exactly call it a holiday for me. I am stuck in the back room with Oliver.

He is virtually an adult, but still very active and irritating at times. Being in his company for long periods has given me an opportunity to observe him closely. I am certain that the difference between us goes well beyond our age and what Tony calls our breeding. Two cats couldn't look or act less alike, and we speak our wonderful Cat Language in distinctly different ways. We talk virtual Cat Dialects. His voice is louder and sharper than mine, and he talks much more. Actually, he can be a pest, talking and complaining all the time. With all of that, I have to admit that he is exceedingly affectionate. Oliver is decidedly more athletic, and gets up to all sorts of tricks that I would not dream of trying. He is Cat Smart too, in almost Human ways that surprise me. He is logical and can calculate how deep a bucket is, and the distance and height of things far faster than I can. Helping, and caring is my main skill.

He is a one person cat, and that person is Tony. He is fiercely loyal to Tony, and adores him. When Tony comes home, Oliver is waiting for him, tail quivering. He is affectionate towards me too, rubbing against me, talking to me, and bopping his head against mine. He does everything in extremes. I am more placid and less temperamental. Thank Cats Above for that!

Rat's Poo! Tony has even trained him to shake paws like a dog!

After a brief break, the huge human workers are back and we are locked up again. Oliver is tense and restless in the small room. When he thrashes his long tail, I recognise signs of his frustration. He wants to run and play, and he becomes a nuisance when he bites my tail or my ear for fun. I give him a sharp slap for that. He has pulled out each tissue from a box, torn the curtain in places, and he is now ripping up the carpet.

He is sending Tony a message, but Tony will pretend he doesn't see it. Oliver can do no wrong, since he won the ribbon at the cat show. I wonder what he will get up to next.

Oliver notices a small mouse dart across the carpet and hide behind the bookcase. A few mice creep into the house through the kitchen door when Karen forgets to close it. I leave it for Oliver to hunt. If he is occupied chasing it, I will have some peace. He sits motionless next to the bookcase and waits. Then we hear it scratching the wood. Oliver is patient, and when a tiny head peeps out, he doesn't move, so as not to alert it. As it edges out further, he stalks it. At last he pounces on the mouse, and has it in his claws. Then a big surprise! He throws it up into the air, catches it, and brings it to me as a gift. I am not hungry and don't fancy the mouse, but I thank him. The creature is dead by now, and we leave it on the floor for Karen to throw away. After catching the mouse he is tired, and goes to sleep.

At last, I can sleep too.

We wake, as the door opens. Pops is paying us a visit.

'I came to see how the two of you are doing here during the renovations.' He strokes us both and talks to us. 'I brought some tuna,' he says, opening the tin. The delicious fish is gone in seconds. He leaves and I go back to sleep.

Cat Contemplation! When I wake, I do some serious thinking about Karen's baby. How long will it take to grow inside her before it comes out? Everything that is Human is slow, so I guess it will be slow growing inside her – and what will it look like?

What will happen to us – to me. Will Karen still have time to feed and love me when the baby comes? Not knowing what will happen is not pleasant.

Oliver is usually more of a worrier and far more emotional than I am, but so far he has not said anything about the baby. Perhaps he doesn't realise that Tony will have less time for him when it arrives.

The banging and loud, whirring noises continue incessantly. The human workers appear to be destroying huge sections of our house. When Karen opens the door to let us out for a quick run, we find new alterations. Oliver is unsettled and returns to the room with his tail down, but I investigate. The front room, which I assume is for the baby, is still a mess.

Stinking Rat's Poo! We are locked into the back room again. We are fed up with this unfair, seemingly endless incarceration. Today, another two Humans with loud voices, heavy footsteps, and powerful body odours that we can even smell in our prison, arrive to fix the power supply in the house. They tell Tony to turn off the heat for the day. The house is plunged into icy cold again with no heat from the vents. We are both miserable and cuddle together.

The warmth is back. When Karen lets us out for a run, we find a soft carpet on the floor of the baby's room. The walls in the room smell strange and shine with clean, brightness. The room is ready. It is now waiting for the baby.

Thank Cats! At last, all the workers have left. Our house is peaceful again, and we can run and play indoors.

We find that our house has changed dramatically. There is a new wall and heavy door in the larger television room with a big, high doorknob. When it is closed, the door creates two separate houses instead of the one we knew. The family's bedrooms are on the front side of the wall and door. On the other side, is the new television room, the kitchen, our back room, and a room for Pops. The house is enormous now.

'Why do you think they are doing this?' I ask Oliver.

'I think the door in the television room is there to lock us out of the bedrooms,' he says.

Sometimes Oliver can be brilliant. The new door is a big Cat Door. When Karen's baby arrives, they are going to lock us out. We will not be able to reach the front of the house.

Karen is slightly rounder now. She is hardly eating, and every morning she holds her head and vomits. She is irritable and becomes angry easily. My best approach is to keep out of her way.

The human baby inside her must be making her sick as it grows. I wonder how long it will take to settle inside her.

The cold weather seems endless. When will it be over? Last year it ended when bright green stems popped out in our garden, and the trees showed off soft, little flowers. Will it be warmer outside when the baby comes out?

At night I've missed sleeping next to Karen on the big bed. My important dreams were on Karen's bed, smelling the perfume of her hair. Sleeping next to her is a beautiful memory now. Since we've been locked out of the bedrooms, I've had only a few dreams I remember. Last night while I cuddled next to Oliver for warmth, I had a weird dream.

I was in the baby's room. There was a baby in the room that looked like a kitten. It was pink and hairless but it had kitten's ears. It mewed loudly and was hungry all the time.

I stood in the room watching it grow. It ate so much that it grew larger and larger and demanded all Karen's attention, while I seemed smaller and smaller. Oliver disliked it and tried to bite it. It was an awful creature that was eating our food, taking over our house and Karen.

Just as well Oliver nudged me and I woke.

'You've been *meowing* in your sleep. Everything okay?' He said.

'Just a nasty dream. I'll go to the kitchen for something to eat and then I'll be fine,' I replied.

The image of the huge baby is still with me today, but I will forget about it. I know that Karen loves me and I must never forget it.

This morning a woman arrives to hang curtains in the baby's room. Yesterday a big parcel arrived. Inside was a small white bed with high sides.

Karen is still working, but she goes out daily between her appointments. When she returns she carries parcels. The baby's room is changing again. Next to the white bed, is a white chair, and there is other white furniture in the room. She allows us into the room to smell everything, but we are not allowed to jump onto the small bed, or on any of the baby's furniture. We mark the corners of the room as our territory, but we know that this room is not ours.

As Karen becomes fatter, our lives keep changing. We have new routines and new rules. When Tony and Karen go to sleep, they lock the big door in the television room to keep us out of the front of the house. During the day, the door to the baby's room is closed unless Karen or Tony are with us.

Oliver is not concerned about the alterations, but I am

certain they will bother him later. On the positive side, Karen and Tony sit with us at night to pet, and play with us.

Karen whispers to me, 'I love you, and you will always be my most beautiful cat, my Bella.'

I will love her always.

Cat's Alive! What in Catland is happening now?

Karen calls us into the baby's room and plays weird, high-pitched sounds for us on the music machine. Our ears are back while we listen. We have never heard sounds like them. We agree that they must be human, calling noises. They do not sound like rabbits, mice, possums, rats or dog sounds. She plays the noises louder some days and softer on other days. We are becoming used to them.

Oliver says, 'They must be baby sounds. Karen is teaching us the noises the new baby will make.'

'I think you're correct,' I tell him.

When we enter the room today, there is something small, pink and new in the little bed. Karen shows it to us. It is plastic, slightly smaller than us, and rounder. It has a head, small body, legs and arms, and it looks Human. She holds it and strokes it. Oliver says it must be similar to the new baby.

Karen has big and small bottles, and new blankets in the room as well. She spreads liquid from a bottle onto her hands and allows us to smell her. She sprinkles white powder that smells like flowers on her body, and then lets us to smell her again.

'She's teaching us how the baby will smell,' Oliver says. 'I wish it would come.'

As Karen grows fatter, she buys toys and tiny clothes, and

puts them in the white cupboard in the baby's room. One of the baby's toys I would like to play with sits above the tiny bed. It has fun objects dangling from it and makes tinkling noises when it shakes.

She is only working a few hours a day now and only calls me occasionally to help in the therapy room. She spends less time on her computer, but more time talking on her small hand phone.

Now Karen is so fat that she can no longer bend. She is tired and complains often that her back hurts. She sits or lies on the couch in the television room most of the day and talks a lot on her phone. Oliver says that she must be in the final stages of waiting for her baby to come out.

I am sitting next to her and I put my head on her huge tummy. I can hear fine beats. I like the sound, purr, close my eyes and sleep. Suddenly a strong kick from inside Karen's tummy wakes me. Karen laughs her happy laugh.

'The baby will be coming out soon', Oliver says knowingly.

Great Cats Alive! It is early morning. I am still asleep, when Tony grabs me and puts me into my carry box. He puts Oliver into his box too. Then we are in the back of Tony's car.

Oliver cries loudly. He dislikes the sensation of the car moving and stopping. He is frightened.

'Shush, Oliver,' Tony says.

I am used to being in a carry box now, but Oliver is not.

The car stops completely. Tony opens the door, and takes us out. I smell the smell of the Cat Prison. Worse, I hear Horrible's voice again. She was my jailor the last time I was here. I cry for the first time. Oliver cries louder.

'Cat's chorus this morning,' 'Horrible' says.

'Put them together in a big cage. It should only be for a day or two. I will let you know,' I hear Tony say, as he leaves. He turns around, looking a little worried about leaving us, and goes.

Big, Rotten, Rats' Poo! He should be worried about leaving us in this awful jail, with this dreadful Human in control. He is doing an unspeakable thing incarcerating us in this awful place, and moving us from our territory, and all we know. It must have something to do with the baby coming out. It has been living inside Karen for a very long time.

Horrible puts us in a large cage together. It has two levels, one for sleeping and another for food and litter. There is only one litterbox to share, but two bowls of food and two of water. Tony has forgotten our baskets so we have to sleep in dirty baskets where other cats have slept before us.

There are many types of cats around us in cages. We feel threatened. They stare and hiss at us, but at least they cannot touch us. This prison is as creepy as it was last time. At least Oliver is with me, but he continues to *meow*.

I try to calm him, but nothing helps. I explain to him that Karen and Tony will not leave us here indefinitely, that they love us, and will be back to collect us. I start the job of rubbing my scent on the cage wire. I call Oliver to help me to make the cage our own, explaining that once our scents are throughout the cage, we will feel better.

The kind young man is not here this time. Horrible is meant to care for us.

Stinking, Dead Rats! Why do we have to put up with Horrible? Surely the management of this prison must realise that she is useless at her job. I sense that she hates all cats. She should definitely be working elsewhere -with dead things.

There isn't much for her to do here except change our

water, litterboxes, and let us out for a short run. The food she gives us is poor quality. As bad as it is, there is not even enough of it to eat – a Cat Crime. What is she doing with it?

Does she think she can get away with stealing our food?

Other cats are complaining loudly. We are all hungry. Everywhere in the cattery unhappiness and restlessness is building. Another miserable night passes and a hungry day with only a short run. She has not turned the heating up high enough and we are all freezing. The disquiet in the cattery is escalating.

Oliver's blue eyes blaze with fury. My fur bristles.

SssssKssssss! Enough! Enough! He says.

'The time has come to do something about Horrible, to take *Cat Action*. The power of many can defeat her,' I tell him.

I begin to yowl, *Meeeeeeoooooow, meeeewoooooow, waaaaaaoooooow, waaawowaaaaa.*

Oliver with his louder, sharper voice joins in. He calls as loudly as his lungs will allow. Siamese yowls are powerful. The other cats hear us and follow our lead. The two Burmese in the cage next to us join in, then the Persian. Soon all the cats are calling, some softly, others louder. As there are about twenty of us in the cattery, the sound is overwhelming. Horrible has no idea how to stop the noise. First she begs us to stop, and then swears at us, but we all ignore her.

Humans outside hear the noise and knock loudly on the door.

'Are you murdering the cats? I will report you to the RSPCA for cruelty,' one shouts. 'Poor kitties,' another calls.

Others who dislike cats demand that something is done to stop the noise.

Eventually, Horrible calls the cattery management for help and an older Human arrives.

'Shush, shush cats,' he says over the din. 'Everything will be alright...shush, shush!' His voice is kind. He rushes to check what is troubling us. 'It's freezing cold in here and all your bowls are empty!' He glares at Horrible. 'And you've been giving the cats poor quality food. What are you up to?'

He turns up the heating and collects new packets of food from a room at the back. Systematically, he fills each of bowl to the top with tastier food. The noise stops.

Thank Cats Above! He tells Horrible that she is sacked.

'I will look after the cats myself until I find a true cat lover to look after them. People leave their beloved animals in our care. If they knew that they were hungry and badly treated they would be terribly upset.'

The man is caring. He talks to each of us, and allows us to run for long periods. We are all calmer and quieter. A day later, a young woman who smells a bit like Karen arrives to care for us. She has a sweet *meow* in her voice. She comes to our cage and talks to us. We let her stoke us and we both purr. Life in incarceration is improving!

We are now accustomed to the routine of our prison. Though the young woman is kind, and loves cats, captivity is unpleasant and stressful. The cats around us are unfriendly, and each complains that they deserve better.

Oliver and I become even closer. We chat, rub and lick each other. We are family, even if we are different, and we are pleased to have each other.

At last, we hear Tony's voice. He has come to collect us. I am angry with him, Oliver is furious. Neither of us greet him with affection. We will not give him the satisfaction of knowing what discomfort and hurt he caused us.

'What's wrong with you two? Aren't you pleased to see me?' He asks.

He puts us in our carry boxes and takes us to the car. This time the journey does not bother Oliver. He knows he is going home, and that is all that matters.

Soon we will have control over our lives again.

Karen is waiting for us. She calls us in her sweet voice, but neither of us go to her. I turn my back on her and Oliver copies me.

Fat Rats! I am going to sulk for a long time.

I search the house systematically for any changes while we were away. The big door leading to the rest of the house is closed. Its knob is high, and harder to reach, than the other knobs on doors throughout the house. The intention I am sure, is to make it impossible for Oliver to open it.

Karen ignores our sulks and offers us chicken. We eat hungrily. I'm angry with myself for giving in so easily and eating the food. My *Cat Scruples* always melt when tasty food is offered.

My love for her dominates. After a few moments of indecision, I go to her. Oliver looks for Tony. When he can't find him, he goes to Karen. She strokes and cuddles us both lovingly and tells us how pleased she is that we are home again.

There are some obvious changes in her. She is slimmer and smells of sweet milk, powder and lotions. I recognise the flowery powder and lotions she encouraged us to sniff earlier.

Then we hear it…. *Wha Whawaaaah! Whawaaaah!* It is an unmistakable sound. It's the sound Karen made us listen to on the music machine before we were taken to prison. It has to be the baby crying.

Wha Whawaaaah!

I look at her questioningly. She lifts a small blanket and allows us to smell it. It has a strange human smell – the smell of the baby.

'Come,' she says to me. She leaves Oliver behind the door and I follow her into the house, to the baby's room. It smells strongly of powder, lotions, and human poo.

'This is our baby. His name is George,' she says.

She picks me up to show me the wrapped, sleeping creature. He is the tiniest Human I have ever seen.

As she places a cover over the baby, she says to me, 'I love you Bella and always will, but I won't have as much time for you as before. George is like a tiny kitten. He has to be fed often and he needs a lot of my attention.'

Then she allows Oliver into the room and talks to him too.

All previous changes in our lives were minor compared to this one. It will have enormous impact on us both.

Spring

Today, a cloudless sky, and rays of gentle sunlight welcome us again, but tomorrow rain and sharp winds may return. The branches of the half-tree are no longer bare but wearing green leaf buds. Grass covers the ground again, flowers pop out of the earth and our catnip is growing abundantly. We are enjoying being more active, sleeping less, and playing outdoors. Bugs, insects and mice are surfacing and we can stalk and catch them once more. What an excellent time to be a cat!

The birds are back, singing in the trees to torment us.

Our tiny bells tinkling to warn them of our presence continue to be an enormous frustration. We have not caught a single bird, and it appears that we will forever be denied of that pleasure. Karen is determined to prevent us killing birds, and she is winning.

Oliver spots a rabbit next door. At first, he thinks it is a cat with long ears, but soon he realises his error. He sits at the fence observing it.

Oliver is a fully-grown cat now. However, he doesn't appear to understand that life is not perfect, and that something big or small could occur to cause him discomfort or disruption at any time. His complaints are about minor alterations in his routine, a rainy day, or if food is not exactly to his liking. Ability to adapt is an important aspect of Catness.

The inside of the house has its challenges. We object strongly to the big door, and to the form the house has taken since George was born. Being locked behind the big Cat Door every night is annoying and upsetting.

I try not to view the door as rejection, or lack of trust. Surely Karen and Tony don't think we would intentionally harm George.

George makes an incredible amount of noise, and his

crying interferes with our sleep. His constant Wha Wha Whaaaa is not at all pleasing to sensitive feline ears. He pees and poos an incredible amount, so that Karen has to clean and change him often.

I hope he grows soon. Then he will be more independent and Karen will have more Cat Time.

Tonight, cool spring winds blow, and rain splatters on the roof like rat droppings. Oliver sniffles and has itchy ears.

'Cats can have hay fever just like humans,' Karen says to Tony, as she strokes Oliver sympathetically.

I shiver and my throat feels sore and blocked. My coughing annoys Oliver. When, to his disgust, he watches me vomiting blobs on the carpet, he is horrified and finds the smell offensive. With his fine, silky coat he has no fur build up with seasonal changes.

For me with my heavier coat, vomiting dead fur is a relief.

In the morning, Karen sees the vomit and mutters about fur balls, but she is not angry if I mess. She cleans it up and sprays the carpet with disinfectant.

'You are moulting with the spring weather. I know you don't vomit on purpose, Treasure,' she says. 'I will brush your coat when I have a free moment.'

She checks on George. 'Oh no, George,' I hear her say. 'You have vomited too...and all over your blanket. It's one of those mornings.'

Sunlight is everywhere today, as we run into our garden. Honey is enjoying the warmer weather, and standing at the fence waiting for us. She barks and wags her tail at me first, and then at Oliver. She is pleased to see us and wants to play. Karen hears the barking and leaves George, to open the fence gate.

'Play nicely,' she says.

Honey races through the gate. I watch her try to chase Oliver, but he is too fast for her. She whines in exasperation. Then I play with her, and pretend to be slower than her. Just when she thinks she has caught up with me, I climb the half- tree. We taunt her until she runs home through the gate. We play together, pouncing, stalking and chasing each other until we drop onto the grass, exhausted. Then we catch up to rub against each other affectionately.

Karen carries George into the television room and sits on the couch with him. We sit together on a comfortable chair, listening and watching, as she talks to him, cuddles, and smiles at him. He has a box filled with toys in different shapes and colours. She chooses a colourful toy and shakes it until he smiles at the movement and noise. Then she tickles him until he makes strange bubbling noises.

Happy Cats! I am pleased for Karen. She is enjoying being a mama, and she adores George.

He is much like a kitten in the way he likes cuddles and tickles. I like watching his small, fat legs kick, and his hands try to grasp things that are not there. He must be doing baby exercises to make his body stronger.

Karen feeds George from her body as my mama fed me. Whenever he cries for food, she feeds him. Once he is satisfied, his eyes close and she puts him to sleep in his little bed. He sleeps even more than I do. She goes to him if he wakes and cries. She tries hard not to let him become distressed. She is a loving mama.

I have to admit to myself that I am jealous of the attention she gives George. I tell myself I am a fortunate adopted cat, and that I must remember that George comes from Karen's body. She is his real mother, and he must be her first love. It is her love that will protect him as he grows. It is from her he will learn about Humanness.

What will George be like when he is bigger? In the same way as cats, Humans take after members of their family, I hope George has Karen's temperament. If he is like Liz, we will have to keep out of his way. In a while, we will find out.

Babies cry when hungry, sleep a lot, and suck food from their mamas like kittens, but kittens are stronger and grow up fast. By the time they are five weeks old, they are almost independent. They can walk and keep warm without their mamas. Soon they begin to eat solid food and drink water. With so many threatening predators about, kittens have to be on their feet early and care for themselves. Even with our smaller size and shorter lives, I would rather be a cat. Humans are such needy creatures.

Tony has changed dramatically. The first change came when Oliver arrived. Now that George is here, he is almost another Human – more patient and gentler. He smiles and laughs a lot. He adores George, even rocks him to sleep and sings to him. I like him more now.

George is asleep and Karen has time for us. She calls me. I am her cat, so I have first choice of a place on her lap, while Oliver puts his head on her thigh. She strokes us both and we feel loved. Then Oliver has a turn of sitting on her lap. I listen to his contented purr, as she cuddles and strokes him.

He is her cat too and deserves affection, but not too much.

It is early morning. The birds are singing, and pink light streams through the window. While George is still asleep, Karen is in the kitchen. She places sandwiches, cakes and biscuits on the big table.

Fat, Rats! Visitors will be coming...again!

The doorbell rings and human mothers pour into our house. Some have brought their babies with them – big and smaller ones. Predictably, we are locked away in the back room, listening to the sounds of babies crying and mothers talking. The sound of so many Humans and their babies invading our house is overwhelming! The noise continues for a few hours. After they all leave the human smell pervades the house and a pile of gifts for George is on the little table.

Thank Cats! Karen opens the windows, cleans and tidies. We then mark the furniture and carpets, restoring our territory.

What a job, but the house is ours again!

Though Karen cleans George many times during the day, he has a bath every night. This is obviously a human ritual, and I am relieved that Karen only forces me into the laundry tub every few months. Unlike me, George enjoys his bath. There are soft ducks in his bath and he plays with them floating in the water.

I think of my friend the duck and wonder if he will come back to play with me. If Oliver attacks him, it may not be such a good idea.

George is a happy baby, who cries only if he is hungry, tired, or needs to be changed. After his bath, he smells of soap, white flowery powder, and is pink all over. Karen kisses his fat tummy, plays with his toes and tiny fingers, and kisses them one by one. She makes bubble sounds for him and he laughs.

She changes his clothes many times due to the messes he makes. He creates a lot of work for her, but she doesn't seem to mind. Some days I watch her comb his hair and choose his tiny clothes to dress him. She says she enjoys him looking "handsome" and "well-dressed."

Everyone's attention is focussed on George. He is lifting his head and smiling at Karen now, and everyone comments that he is becoming stronger. He notices Oliver, and me too. His tiny hands reach out towards us and he makes strange noises. Watching this small Human grow is intriguing.

While Oliver is in the garden playing, Karen calls me. She puts George on his blanket on the carpet and allows me to sniff him, and sit near him. He is not like a kitten any longer. Close to him, I smell his skin and listen to the sounds of his rhythmic breathing. Now his breaths come slower than they did when he was a tiny baby.

Karen trusts me with him, as I lie close to him and purr. I like this little creature. Then she calls Oliver, and he approaches George slowly. He smells him and purrs too. Now George has a cat on each side of him, and he looks happy.

Liz and Pops visit often. As grandparents, they both want to see George. They play with him, hold him, and kiss him all over. They smile when they are with him, and are happy just watching him.

Liz buys George gifts of toys and clothing. Karen is pleased and thanks her, but I sense subtle vibrations of tension between Karen and her mother.

Today Liz looks concerned.

'You have a baby…and two cats. I know you won't like

what I say. Cats can be dangerous around small children... and they can pass on diseases.'

'Tony and I are extremely careful,' Karen replies. We love George and our cats. Tony changes and cleans their litterboxes and washes his hands thoroughly afterwards.'

Liz purses her lips disapprovingly.

'We watch the cats when they are with George, so try not to worry about it. Anyway, gentle animals are good for a baby.'

'I belong to the old school. No dogs or cats near young children.'

Karen's relief when her mother leaves is obvious. Her relationship with Pops is more open and friendly. He is besotted with "Georgie", as he calls him.

Pops tickles George's tummy and then lifts him up high. George chuckles with joy, wanting more...and more.

After playing with George, Pops finds us.

'Bella, remember me telling you how I longed for a grandchild. Now that he is here my life is so full and happy.'

I butt his head affectionately and purr.

He smiles. 'I made a special gift for the two of you. I know it isn't much fun right now with Tony at work and Karen so involved with the baby.'

We wait for the special gift while he goes outside to collect it. He carries in a large, complex wooden concoction with tunnels and climbing platforms.

Cat's Delight! We can barely wait until it is on the floor to play on it. Just as well it is strong and can take our weight. Pops is thrilled to see us both having fun. He laughs as he watches Oliver jump up to the tallest platform.

'When George is older, and Bella is working with Karen again, I will enter you, Oliver, in another cat show. You are a handsome cat, and I'm sure that this time you will win the top neutered adult category.'

Oliver's tail drops and he runs under the table to hide.

George is growing fast. He has dark hair like Karen's and a nose like Tony's. His eyes seem to be turning brown. He smiles at me, laughs, and says *Coo Coo.* I like him more each day. His little limbs are stronger now, and he moves on the floor. Karen says he is crawling. He is still almost like a little animal, but I expect he will try to stand soon. Now that he is bigger, I rub my head against his tiny hand and he reaches out to touch me.

During the day, we run through the entire house as we once did. Life has almost returned to the pleasant routine before he arrived. Karen has stopped feeding him, and he is eating mushy food from bottles.

Meeyuk! His food smells awful. A kitten wouldn't touch it!

Karen hasn't started working yet, but I can tell that she is bored. She paces and looks for things to do when George is asleep. She cleans, bakes cakes and biscuits, or cooks Tony special meals. Cooking and cleaning did not interest her at all while she was working.

This afternoon, Karen takes George with her to visit a friend, and we are alone in the house. Oliver has "itchy paws" again. He cannot resist trying to open the big door in the television room. He has the length and strength to reach all the lower knobs and handles in the house, and can open doors and cupboards. After several tries, he is able to reach the doorknob in the television room, but he will have to practice a lot before he can open it.

He is smart, and strong, but his rebelliousness and risk taking concerns me.

The half-tree is covered in new leaves and the flowers in our garden are attracting bees and butterflies. I have learned that bees are to be avoided. They seem to particularly enjoy stinging cat's noses and ears. Butterflies are fun to stalk and catch.

Oliver is chasing me around the garden, when I hear a familiar whirring sound. I stop to look up. Two dark blobs are hovering above us. A surge of excitement throbs within me. The duck is back, and with a friend. They land on our fence and watch us.

My thrill is mixed with concern. Will Oliver consider them prey and stalk them?

I don't have long to wait to find out. He is preparing to attack them.

Meooooow...ow!

'No Oliver! They are ducks...my friends.'

Thank Cats Above! He is displeased, but retreats to observe them.

Quark, quark they say in unison.

Meow, meow I reply.

I recognise the markings of my old friend as it flies towards me, teasing me. I run after it chasing it behind the rocks. Then it is high up on the half-tree. I climb the tree but it is too fast for me. While Oliver watches us play, the second duck flies behind him and tweaks his ear. Oliver turns, but the duck is above him, tempting him to follow and play. Soon we are both playing with the ducks and having fun.

Karen has returned and is watching us play.

She laughs loudly. 'So, your duck friend is back with a pal for Oliver. You are both hilarious!'

Oliver has been practicing reaching the doorknob in the television room each night. This afternoon while Karen is out again, he runs to the big door and after several attempts at turning it, gives a loud, *meoooow* of success. The door is open.

He races through the house. As hard as I try to resist the temptation, I follow. We run back and forth until we are tired. Then we return to the back of the house. We cannot close the door, and wait worriedly for Karen's return.

'I was in such a hurry to go out, and with so much to do for George, that I must've forgotten to close the door,' she says. 'You're such good cats for staying on this side of the house.'

I look at Oliver, and then turn away.

The moon is full tonight. Oliver and I sit at the window. Our senses are sharp. We listen to the creatures of the night and enjoy the delicate perfumes of flowers.

Oliver is restless. 'I wish I could go out,' he says.

'Calm down,' I reply and flick him with my tail.

He glares at me with eyes that have a red glow at night.

Neutering has calmed him, but it has not changed him. I hope that he is not considering running away again.

In frustration, he claws at the gift Pops built for us. I pretend not to notice.

'For fun I'm going to open the big door to the bedrooms. I need to run around. They are asleep and won't hear me.'

His eyes shine mischievously, as his long, powerful body

stretches to the doorknob. I hear him turn the knob, and then the pulse of him running.

This time, I do not follow him. In his present mood he could cause big trouble.

I drift off to sleep. When I feel him shaking me, I wake with a start.

'You have to come...quickly! Something is the matter with George,' he says, sounding panicky.

'Are you sure?'

'Hurry! Karen and Tony are asleep...and I don't know what to do.'

We race to George's room. His door is open. I stand next to his little bed and listen. George is making gasping noises. I jump onto his bed, and listen more closely. I have heard him breathing many times. His breaths usually come rhythmically, but now he is struggling to breathe.

Major Cat Alarm! 'I am going to wake them,' I tell Oliver. In seconds, I leap onto the big bed. First I jump on Karen and then on Tony, attempting to rouse them.

Meeeooooow, Meeeooooow I call.

'I want to sleep...leave me alone,' Karen says.

I stamp on her, and then take the sheet in my mouth and pull it from her.

'What's up Bella?' She says sleepily.

Cat Emergency! Hurry up Karen, or Georgie will pass over the rainbow!

By now, Karen is sitting up.

I jump up onto the bed and slap Karen's face with my paw. Then I run towards George's room calling all the time. She follows me.

'To...nee! Come quickly, George is very pale and struggling to breathe. Call the ambulance,' she shouts.

Tony looks at George, and picks up the phone. Soon there is a horrific wailing noise. A huge white van pulls up. Two

Humans run into the house. At first, they are in the room with George, and then they carry him to the van. We hear the loud wailing sound again, as they drive away. Karen and Tony dress in a hurry. They leave as well.

Oliver and I wait through the night and most of the next day. At last, we hear Karen's car in the driveway. She rushes into the kitchen to give us food and water, and change our litterboxes. Then she runs to the bedroom. She has a quick shower, dresses and is gone again. Tony arrives a few hours later. He has a shower, changes his clothes and leaves.

We sleep and wait.

Karen and Tony are away for another night and a day. When they return they are exhausted, but look relieved. They stand in the television room, hug each other, and cry.

'Georgie will be fine...just a few more days in hospital,' Tony says to Karen reassuringly.

Thank Cats Above! George will recover and grow to be a big and strong Human. He survived, so he has the Human equivalent of Catness – Humanness.

Karen wipes away tears and kisses Tony. 'I don't know what would've happened if Bella...and Oliver....'

'Where are the cats?' Tony asks.

We run towards them, and greet them with loud purrs.

Tony wipes tears from his eyes with his sleeve.

'If Oliver hadn't learned to open the big door...and hadn't realised George wasn't well...I don't want to think what could've happened. It was Bella, who knew he was having trouble breathing and woke us. Our cats are incredible... amazing!' He bends to stroke Oliver and then me. 'I doubt either of you understand what I am saying, but you two saved George's life by alerting us.'

Karen and Tony sit on the couch and we jump onto their

laps. It is a glorious love fest, followed by tins of prawns for us...and nibbles of dried beef.

Happy, Happy Cats! George is home in two days. At first, he is in his bed, and he sleeps most of the time. Later, his doctor says he can be up for a short while and play. We are both pleased to have him back with us.

Life is perfect in Catland.

The sunlit mornings are warm, fallen blossoms cover the ground in our garden forming a carpet of luscious, pink softness.

George is walking and beginning to talk. 'Bell' he calls me, and 'Ol' is for Oliver.

Catland couldn't be a happier place.

'Bella, it's time we started work again,' Karen says, giving my head a loving pat. 'Jenny will look after George, while we are busy in the therapy room. We'll start work tomorrow morning, Precious.'